"Acclaimed filmmaker Quentin Lee's novel, *The Secret Diary of Edward Ng*, is cinematic, spare, and devastating in its portrayal of a young man in search of his identity. This novel brutally exposes the lonely spaces between family members and lovers as the story moves from Hong Kong and California. Intensely readable and memorable."

— Naomi Hirahara, Edgar Award-winning author of *Clark and Division*

"The Secret Diary of Edward Ng explores the most universal of themes: Love and Family. In this endearing coming-of-age novel, Quentin Lee gives us a full portrait of a young man's emotional and sexual awakening. It is a story if 1990s Queer Asian life filled with the complexities of AIDS, identity, and full-blown curiosity. A remarkable achievement."

— Noel Alumit, Los Angeles Times bestselling author of *Letters to Montgomery Clift*

"Quentin Lee's novella is a raw, joyful, irreverent depiction of queer Asian-American youth. From his gleeful opening sentence to its final words, his hero takes us on a breathless ride through the pressures of a Cantonese upbringing, the struggle to define his identity as an Asian-American and a gay man, and the joys and perils life can offer and throw at him. Uncompromising and unapologetic, *The Secret Diary of Edward Ng* may or may not be autobiographical, but it demands to be read as a unique new voice in Asian-American Literature."

— Adi Tantimedh, author of The Ravi PI Series

"The Secret Diary of Edward Ng is an audacious and clear-eyed portrait of "becoming Gaysian" in the age of AIDS. Lee conjures a cast of fierce and promiscuous Asian American college students—anchored by the irreverent Edward—while spinning a moving coming of age narrative that could only transpire amid the magic mists of the Bay Area."

— David L. Eng, author of *Racial Melancholia, Racial Dissociation*

"Written in beautifully cinematic language, Quentin Lee's *The Secret Diary of Edward Ng* narrates a queer coming-of-age saga through fearless self-searching, sharpened senses and tangible feelings connected across the Hong Kong-US diaspora. Nostalgic but not sentimental, set in culturally diverse San Francisco during the AIDS era, the story bursts with the hubris of youthful vitality, and resonates perfectly today."

— Shi-Yan Chao, author of *Queer Representations in Chinese-language Film and the Cultural Landscape*

"Edward Ng is one of the most honest persons I've read in fiction. Not only because he doesn't hide anything in front of others but also he never lies to himself which is such a radical choice of lifestyle. Edward Ng's story is not only valuable from an Asian Queer perspective but important for any complex identities which now apply to almost everybody. I see this book as a treasure box of Quentin, he is so generous to share with the readers. I hope you also enjoy it."

— Popo Fan, Chinese Film Director

"Quentin Lee's "The Secret Diary of Edward Ng" follows its titular protagonist Edward Ng, an ambitious, soon-to-be Berkeley graduate. Much of the novel deals with the moral ambiguities facing Edward in his life; the story unfolds in such a way without ever being prescriptive or didactic. Edward must simply make the hard decision to attend grad school as he must also reconcile with the confusion of his intellectual and sexual coming-of-age. Edward's life is at times contemptible as it is redeemable— what could be called a kind of bildungsroman. Indeed he is a troubled young man who must navigate his many, at times, salacious, and estranged relationships, be it with his mother, lover, cousin, uncle and more. His story is mixed in with all that is the feeling of displacement, melancholia, reconciliation and sexual promiscuity, amid the political realities of the 90s and the HIV/AIDS crisis. Through this, Lee conjures the necessary nostalgia of a period that is, in many ways, being left behind for the new."

— Bee Vang, Actor and Activist

"Quentin Lee's preoccupations with gay romance, Chinese folklore, and horror movies can be found in this engaging story of extended family, food, friendship, and erotic entanglements in the queerscape between Hong Kong and Asian America. Semen and sentiment, coming-of-age and coming out, sex-for-sale and liberated love, the novel expands this noted film director's creative vision from the cinema screen to the written word."

— Gina Marchetti, Author of *The Chinese Diaspora on American Screens: Race, Sex, and Cinema*

"Quentin Lee's 'Secret Diary of Edwang Ng' is a raw, passionate and probing novel about being queer Asian against stereotypes of queerness and Asian American-ness. The protagonist occupies a subject position that can be tentatively called a postcolonial queer, whose sensibilities are crisscrossed by multiple power relations in multiple locations. Lee nuances the landscape of queerness with irony, melancholia, nonchalance, and creative abandon all at once."

— Shu-mei Shih, Author of *The Lure of the Modern: Writing Modernism in Semicolonial China*

"Quentin Lee's stylish debut novel, The Secret Diary of Edward Ng, undresses Hong Kong and U.S. society from the vantage of a new generation of sexually experimental youth. Lee brings his considerable skills as a feature filmmaker to his depiction of transnational families on the brink. Poignant moments interspersed with provocative sexuality give this novel an edge that takes you to the millennium."

— Russell Leong, Author of *Asian American Sexualities: Dimensions of Gay and Lesbian Experience*

"His debut novel is as exciting as his films—raw, passionate and trendy all at once."

— *XY Magazine*

"Lee captures the passion, urgency and confusion that Ng experiences in bold passages…"

— *Asianweek*

THE
SECRET
DIARY
OF
EDWARD NG

The Secret Diary of Edward Ng

Quentin Lee

Troublemaker Press

CINCINNATI, OHIO

2021 Troublemaker Press

Publisher's Note: *The Secret Diary of Edward Ng* is a work of fiction. Any resulting resemblance to persons living or dead is entirely coincidental and unintentional.

The Secret Diary of Edward Ng/ Quentin Lee – 1ˢᵗ ed.

Author Photo: Ines Laimins

Cover Layout and Design: Simon Tam

Library of Congress Cataloging-in-Publication Data has neem applied for.

ISBN: 978-1-7336291-8-8 (ebook)

ISBN: 978-1-7336291-9-5 (paperback)

To Mike

In memory of Julian C. Boyd

1

To Ride a Cow

"What do you think I'm writing?" asks Edward with his finger dripping with cool semen.

"Let me feel it." David closes his gray eyes and wets his dry lower lip. He focuses on the ticklish sensations on his chest. "My last name, Wong."

"Very good." Edward smiles and writes the next character of David's Chinese name. "Your penis is so white, like your skin."

"I'm sorry," mutters David, self-conscious. His father has said the same thing. Not about his penis of course. About his skin. That it's always very pale like a white man's.

Half a white man to be precise.

"No, I think it's cute." Edward finishes the last character of David's Chinese name. Before his finger dries, he sticks it in his mouth and tastes the semen mixture between the two of them.

"There's this Chinese hero. I forgot his name. But his mother embroidered four words on his chest, something like be loyal and faithful to the country. He grew up and became a great warrior, but he was betrayed by corrupt officials. When they were about to execute him, they tore open his garment and found those words on his chest."

"And?"

"They just laughed and beheaded him, I suppose." Edward inches his lips close to David's. They kiss. Edward nestles beside David and tucks his chin under the paler jaw.

"Why did you tell me that?"

"I don't know. It came into my mind when I was writing your Chinese name. Somewhat of a literary allusion."

"You're a random boy."

"We don't have to make sense all the time. Sometimes it's just fun to say whatever. You know what I mean?"

"Hm…"

"Do you think before saying everything you say?"

"Is this a trick question?"

"No. Cuz I don't."

"But that's what I like about you."

Silence.

"Let's turn off the lights."

"Okay."

Darkness now. Trying to avoid falling off the edge, two bodies struggled to fit on the twin-sized mattress.

"You like to watch me giving you blow jobs," says Edward in the dark.

"Doesn't it turn you on?"

"Kind of."

"Kind of?"

"As long as it turns you on." He inches his face closer to David's. Another kiss? Perhaps not. He probably doesn't like kissing as much as simply the stretch of intimacy before. Like cum, the kiss somewhat signifies the death of the intimacy.

David shifts to one side. Edward wraps an arm around David's chest. He starts feeling David's soft nipple which hardens after a few more strokes.

"Aren't you sleepy?" asks David.

"Not really. Are you?"

"Uh hm…" mumbles the groggy voice.

He pecks David on the nape and shifts away. David is always sleepy after sex. The gentleness, that will soon expire in daylight, leaks from David's skin. Edward tries to absorb as much as he can now.

"David?"

"Hm?"

"Are you bored with me?"

The rustling of bed sheets.

A soft hand touches Edward's smooth leg. Despite the absence of verbal reassurance, David communicates through a pat, or a touch. Perhaps even another kiss?

"I'm a cow, aren't I?" asks Edward.

Somewhat of a Chinese proverb: *Ride a cow to find a horse. It's still better than walking.*

"You're my little pony," mumbles David. "But *I'm* your cow."

"Let's say we're both cows. A cow fucking another cow."

"Or we're both horses."

Edward first met David in a bisexual rap group two years ago. Now, Edward is 100% gay while David is still bisexual. They hadn't started sleeping together until a few months ago, after Edward painfully gave up on that straight Filipino guy whom he was desperately in love with.

Let's rewind further… In the very "beginning," Edward liked David, but David was seeing some guy named Ricardo. Then some time later, David told Edward that he wanted him, but by that time Edward was so in love with someone else. Some time passed. After talking and procrastinating about having sex for a month, Edward finally convinced David to have a non-exclusive relationship with his current girlfriend, Marlene.

The shrill ring of the telephone tears the silence. Frantic fumbling through the sheets. Edward crawls past David. His palms land on the floor. The telephone lies somewhere in the darkness. Soiled sheets of Kleenex… sharp corners of books… clothes… The answering machine picks up the call. Edward's hand finds the cordless phone buried under a mangled copy of Foucault's *The Use of Pleasure*.

"Hello, hello," Edward tries to talk over his recorded voice.

A little annoyed, David sits up on the bed.

"Edward?"

"It's kind of late." Edward recognizes the voice of his cousin Victor.

"Dad's in critical condition. We're at the St. Francis Hospital. Will you come?"

The lights dawn on the squalid studio. Edward and David sort out their commingled clothes on the floor. Edward zips up his jeans and throws on a T-shirt. In silence, they sit side by side on the bed, putting on their socks and shoes.

"You don't have to go with me."

"Do you want me to go?"

"Yeah. Can you drive?"

As he hands his car keys to David, he notices how the pale skin makes visible the reddish spots and green veins on David's palm. Four or five years ago, he might have traded his soul to be white. But now, after the political re-education at Berkeley, he can't help but look at whiteness with disdain.

Is he attracted to David's Chineseness or his whiteness, or precisely the hybridity? At first glance, he thought David looked very Chinese, yet after holding David's body and tasting his penis, Edward notices the difference. David has a similar body and smell of other Caucasian men whom he has slept with.

"Are you okay?"

Edward opens his eyes. David is driving beside him. They are now crossing the Bay Bridge. The car glides past the connecting sections of the bridge, those momentary jerks amidst the otherwise smooth ride. In the distance, Edward sees the glowing San Francisco skyline shrouded with fog.

"I'm sorry. I fell asleep."

"You don't have to apologize."

"I really don't want to drag you into this." Edward is too exhausted to play the game of cool indifference. "But I want you to come because I don't want to be alone with them."

"Hm."

"My uncle is always pissed when I bring someone home to 'the family dinner.' He always complains that because I bring someone home we can't talk about family matters."

"So I'm there just to piss them off when your uncle is supposed to be in critical condition?"

"No," says Edward. "Why do you think I'm so vengeful?"

"I thought you hated his guts."

"I just need support." Edward turns to the fogging up window and hears David turning up the fan to defog the windscreen. "You don't understand how alone I felt when I lived with them."

"You told me all that."

"I'm sorry that you're here, but I asked you if you minded."

"You don't have to get upset."

"I'm not upset." Edward bites his lower lip. "Sometimes I think you can be mean."

David lays a hand on Edward's shoulder and strokes him gently.

As a child, Edward always liked to play the part of the monster. He would chase his cousin around wearing a werewolf mask. Two years younger, his cousin would be screaming and running. Then his uncle would yell at Edward: *Stop scaring my son!* Edward would take off his mask with a boisterous grin… "It's just a game." His cousin would be giggling too.

"What kind of a game is this? What if I come to your bed in the middle of the night and strangle you?" His uncle's voice echoes in his mind. "Do you think that's funny?"

"I *am* vengeful," says Edward. "I always wished he'd die when I was living with him. I hated him, because he never thought that I'd become anyone, because he made me feel like the black sheep of the family. And I always said to myself: one day you'd see. I'd be well off and better than you ever could be. You'd regret not believing in me."

Early morning. About ten years ago. Edward's *amah* knocked softly on the door. The eleven-year-old boy had been awake for quite some time, almost an hour before he was supposed to wake up. She poked her head through the crack of the door as he sat up with his eyes perfectly open.

"Breakfast is ready."

"I'll come."

Just as the door was about to close—

"Foon Che… I've something to tell you."

With a smile on her face, the fifty-year-old woman approached. Her meaty butt landed beside the boy's scrawny legs. She stroked his lap, desperately trying to suppress her brimming sadness.

He leaned his head against Foon Che. Her wrinkled hand touched the smooth skin over his forehead. Her fingers gently sculpted his hair. She felt the hair, which she had washed and combed for almost eleven years, for one last time. Edward wanted to cry, but he didn't want to make Foon Che feel bad. So he didn't. He knew she was a sentimental woman, because she cried even when she was watching those melodramatic black-and-white Cantonese movies on TV.

"I don't want to go."

"You'll go to Disneyland and have *ghost kids* as friends. When you come back you'll speak English sounding *klacklacklack* and I won't even understand you." She forced out a smile.

The door opened after a few brisk knocks. Edward's mother was standing at the doorway with the back of her dress unzipped. She looked at her son, then at the old maid with a definite jealousy. The boy was closer to some dumb old uneducated woman she hired than to her who gave him birth.

"Foon Che, come help me zip up this dress."

"Coming, *siu nai*,"

Edward watched Foon Che rise from the bed.

"Get dressed and come out for breakfast."

Alone in the room, Edward got up. His clothes for the day were hung on the doorknob of the closet. He took off his pajamas. Neatly he folded them—first the shirt, then the pants—into a rectangle, as Foon Che taught him. Having stuffed his pajamas inside the suitcase, he sat on it to close it.

Foon Che had prepared crepes filled with sweet condensed milk, Edward's favorite, for breakfast. Edward had little appetite, yet he ate everything because he wanted to show his appreciation. His mother was all dressed in a tight white dress. Wearing her usual inch-thick layer of make-up, she asked the boy some questions to which he answered laconically.

The phone rang. It was his best friend—a boy named Lee Man Wai. They were friends since first grade, and they had vowed to marry each other when they grew up. He told his mother about how much he wanted to marry Lee Man Wai. She told him that he could only marry a girl. Why? His mother told him that he would know "why" when he grew up.

Paulina was his mother's name. She was holding his silky hand in the back seat while the chauffeur drove silently, occasionally catching Paulina's tearful eyes in the rearview mirror. Edward leaned his head against her shoulder, pretending to miss her but actually missing others.

Grandmother (Edward's deceased father's mother) didn't go to the airport because she never got along with Paulina, that fickle woman. But she saw Edward the night before, and gave him a "red pocket" with five hundred U.S. dollars and a jade amulet on a 24K gold necklace.

"Will you miss Mom?" Paulina patted her eyes softly with a Kleenex.

"Probably."

Silence. She was sobbing in a suppressed manner that he found irritating.

"Why do I have to go?" He had been asking the question again and again since her decision a year ago. At first it was charged with accusation and anger. Then, in the last few months, it became the voice of a Chinese ghost, the constant repetition in spite of the knowledge of futility, as if that would drive her to madness.

"You'll thank me for it, Chung Tuck, trust me."

"And you're going to marry Mr. Clifford?"

Mr. Clifford was the man with whom she disappeared night after night.

"Don't be stupid." She sniffled her nose.

"You've already forgotten Pa."

"I have to live too. After you're gone, I'll be so lonely. Your mother needs friends too."

Edward turned away and looked out of the window. The car entered the cross-harbor tunnel, heading toward the airport on the Kowloon island. Edward observed the walls of the tunnel for one last time. They were covered with huge rectangular brown slabs which a much younger Edward used to think were chocolate chunks.

At the airport, Paulina started arguing with a bitchy woman at the United Airlines counter because all the non-smoking seats had been taken. *But he's a kid, he's only eleven, it's hazardous to his health...* Standing beside his mother and the huge suitcases, Edward felt lost and irritated. He tried telling her that he didn't care if he sat beside a smoker, but she refused to hear him until the woman finally found a non-smoking seat for her momentarily precious little prince.

Alone at last and glad to be free of his mother's melodrama, Edward stepped inside the restricted area which permitted only boarding passengers. He was carrying a canvas travel bag over his bony shoulder with his British Hong Kong passport in his hand. With a timid voice, he answered the questions of the immigration officer.

An hour after the plane took off, he felt despair. He could see the clouds outside the window, and he was now in the middle of the sky. There could be no return unless he killed the pilot and turned the plane around. But he was too weak to even speak. He could no longer conjure up his imaginary friends who *might* rescue him because reality was so oppressive.

Chilled night wind blows against them as they gallop up the steps toward the main entrance of the hospital. David holds Edward's hand.

Their sneakers squeak on the gray linoleum floor as they walk slower and deeper into the hospital. They stop beside the hospital room. Edward's cousin Victor and Aunt Linda are sitting with their backs against the incoming visitors.

"Hi."

Victor and Linda turn around, almost in unison. They are silent. Edward disengages his hand from David's.

"How's Uncle?" He steps toward his kin.

The man is lying on the cot beside an ECG monitor and an IV. Now he is just a pale balding man with a pudgy stomach under the white hospital sheet.

David stands stiffly a few feet from the four *pure* Asians. He hears them exchange a few lines of Cantonese. Linda and Victor cast a cold glance at him. Tucking his hands in his shorts pockets, he surveys the room with his tired but no longer sleepy eyes. He feels irritated, but he realizes that he should be sympathetic. He looks at the Chinese-mumbling people and feels their subtle conspiracy and his lack of connection, not only in blood but in culture.

Edward beckons David to approach. David shakes hands with the unenthusiastic woman and the cute but unfriendly cousin. After a few more minutes of silence, Victor whispers something to Edward and they rise from the chairs.

"I'll be back," Edward whispers to David.

In the cold and bleakly lit corridor, Edward and Victor, two years apart, walk side by side. Heads down, they stop beside a water fountain where Victor bends down and puts his mouth next to the spout. Edward stands silently with his arms crossed.

"Do you want any?"

"I'm not really thirsty."

"Why did you bring him?"

"I don't know."

"You're really an insensitive person."

"Insensitive about what?"

"Fuck you, Edward. Sometimes you can really piss people off, you know that? It's not the time and place, you get it?"

Silence.

"He's my father, and I love him."

"I understand," says Edward meekly. "Why did you call if you knew that he cared nothing for me? I'm of no importance to your father."

"You're part of the family, whether you hate us or not. I treat you as my brother, and my mom treats you as her son."

Mocked and touched, Edward is silent.

While the two Chinese boys are negotiating, David sits silently beside Linda. He watches the monotonous pattern of the cardiogram. He hears her breathing and occasionally shifting in the chair beside him, yet he dares not turn to face her.

Thanks, Edward.

"What's your name again?" asks Linda.

"David."

"You go to Berkeley too?"

"Yes." Pause. "I'm really sorry about all this."

She forces out a smile. She can't be angry at the kid. Yeah, they're just kids, and they think they need to prove themselves with their rudeness and all. She could think of a thousand ways to forgive people, including Edward, her son and her husband. For all these years, she has aspired to be a patient parent and an understanding wife.

"So the two of you are going out?" asks Linda.

"Yeah, I guess so."

"Well." Pause. "I'm happy if Edward finds someone he loves. Someone stable. We worry a lot about him. Especially because he's… you know."

"Don't worry. We're safe."

Linda nods.

Some night during Edward's junior year in high school. They must be having some kind of pasta since his uncle owned and operated a pasta factory then. He would bring home boxes after boxes of pasta, which meant pasta five nights a week. While they were having dinner, the telephone rang. Aunt Linda grabbed the cordless phone. It was for Edward.

"Tell him he'll call back," said his uncle with a mouthful of pasta.

Edward watched his aunt hang up. She returned to her seat at the dining table and picked up the fork.

"It's Olivia," said Aunt Linda. "She said she's not home, but she'll call you back."

Edward took a sip of water, then he said abruptly, "I'm supposed to meet her for a movie in an hour."

"She'll call back," said his uncle.

"Yeah, but why couldn't I talk to her in the first place, so I would save her the trouble?"

"Because you're having dinner."

"Let's eat," said Aunt Linda with a pacifying glance at her nephew.

"You're so arbitrary," Edward muttered under his breath and picked up the fork.

Silence.

"I'm just trying to teach you manners, which your mother has never taught you," said his uncle. "She sent you here for an education, and I'm precisely responsible for that. I don't want to see you become a bum on the street."

Olivia never called back that night even though Edward waited and waited with expectation. At eleven, his curfew time, Edward crawled into bed without saying goodnight to his uncle.

Victor shuffled out of the bathroom in his pajamas and slippers, and switched off the lights. "Night," he said to his sulky older cousin and hopped into bed. Noises of bodies shifting under blankets. Rustling of bed sheets.

"I'm sorry she didn't call," said Victor softly.

"I don't care."

"Are you mad at Dad?"

"I hate him."

Darkness. Sounds of night insects from outside. Just as Victor closed his eyes, he heard Edward sobbing. It wasn't the first time.

"Some day I'll leave. I swear," muttered Edward in a tearful voice.

"You'll go away for college."

"Yeah…" A few more minutes passed. "Can I sleep with you tonight?"

Around six in the morning… His uncle remains unconscious, but the doctor has assured them that the man would be fine. They're crossing the Bay Bridge once again. This time they are under the bridge. The stretch from San Francisco toward East Bay is uniform and viewless.

"This is my favorite part of the drive," says David, driving through a short tunnel lit with orange lights.

"The tunnel?"

"Don't you think this is a neat tunnel in the middle of a boring bridge?"

The tunnel ends. They return to a stretch similar to that before the tunnel. Edward looks at the moving reflections at the top of the windshield and closes his eyes.

"I don't think it's boring," says Edward. "I think it's comforting, because it's all the same." Pause. "So what do you think about my cousin?"

"He's cute."

"Yeah." He can't help suppressing a smile because he knows that David would find his cousin cute.

"You really hate your uncle, don't you?"

"I guess I hate him."

"Is that why you slept with your cousin?"

"Is that what you think of me?"

"It only seems logical."

"Do you think I'm really that utilitarian? That everything I do and everyone I fuck has to be of use to me?"

"I wouldn't know."

With a teasing smile, he fondles David's lap and squeezes the warm bulge throbbing under garment. "Why are you useful to me?"

"I'm your free chauffeur."

"So that's it, ha."

Edward bends down and unzips David's shorts. He licks the trapped hardness behind the thin garment of David's underwear. David keeps his eyes on the road and tousles Edward's hair as Edward releases David's penis out of the piss slit on the briefs.

"Drive carefully," says Edward and starts sucking.

The funeral of his father took place three days after the fatal car accident. Edward cried, not so much because of his father but more because of his grandmother, his *amah*, his mother and his relatives who were all crying. About a hundred people attended the funeral. Friends, colleagues and relatives all came to pay respect. It was considered tragic, since his father was only a little over thirty at his death.

Paulina had insisted on a Chinese funeral. A group of Buddhist nuns were hired to chant for the dead man. Although Edward's grandmother would have preferred a less ceremonious event, she didn't argue with Paulina. After all, what was there to argue about? Her son was dead.

All in white, Edward was cushioned between his mother and his grandmother, two strong women with tears in their eyes. Every now and then, he would scoot beside his *amah*, Foon Che, who was burning dead people's money with one hand and wiping the tears from her eyes with the other.

Lee Man Wai had also come to the funeral with his parents. The boy was dressed in a white shirt and black pants. Edward watched his friend and his parents bow once, twice and thrice before his father's black-and-white photograph. Man Wai stole a glance at Edward and followed his parents to the guest seated on the other side of the room. Forbidden to meet in the ceremonious atmosphere, the two seven-year-old boys were thinking of each other in the same room.

After the funeral, the coffin was transported to the grave for burial. Fearing that Edward might be tired, his grandmother sent him home with Foon Che. To his grandmother's prediction, he fell asleep on the drive home.

When he woke up again, he was in his own bed and the sky outside the window was dark. For a moment he thought that the funeral and all was a dream. He got up from the bed and slipped out of his room. Streaks of moonlight were projected on the floor of the living room. His father's photograph was sitting on the dining table among other stuff that he could not make out in the dark.

The kitchen tiles felt icy on his bare feet. He opened a jar of dried beef jerky. He left the kitchen nibbling on a slice of beef jerky. His stomach a little more filled, he washed away the soy sauce on his fingers and went back to bed.

Father was dead.

Edward realized that he should cry, but he couldn't understand why he did not feel like crying. He had watched Japanese cartoons in which parents would die and leave a child orphaned. The child was then sent to an orphanage. Or perhaps, one of the parents died, and the living one remarried an evil stepfather or stepmother. It was tragic, and he felt sad for those children.

Thinking of the cartoon orphans, he was beginning to feel pitiful. Soon he was sobbing under the blanket. Tears rolled down his eyes. He thought of all the things that they could have done together. He thought of the Mercedes sports car that he would never ride again. He imagined the collision—glass shattering, blood flowing from his father's wounds, the metal deforming.

For a brief moment he saw his father's corpse in the coffin. A flash of memory from the funeral: his father's reconstructed face.

Edward believed in ghosts since he loved American horror movies and old Cantonese movies. If his father's ghost was standing there, right beside his bed, he wondered how he would feel. Should he be afraid? Should he feel protected?

When his father was alive, he scarcely saw him during the week since he spent most of his time in the office. At five years old, Edward still had the hope of seeing his parents before bedtime. He would try to stay up later and later, watching television with Foon Che. Every so often he would see his father and mother entering the front door. They would greet him, give him a kiss on the cheek or a pat on the head, and quickly retreat to their room.

When he entered primary school, he made a best friend and learned to be less dependent on his parents' affection. He would chat on the phone with Lee Man Wai until he went to bed. Of course, there was TV and Foon Che to entertain him.

Stuffed animals, Japanese model cars and Transformers filled the shelves of his bedroom. They were all that his father left to him: mass-produced tokens of capitalism.

Four days have passed. His uncle has been brought home for recovery. Edward calls his uncle up to wish him well. His uncle invites him over for dinner and then passes the phone to his cousin. Victor says coldly, *No David…*

Edward calls David next.

"What are you doing?"

"Not much."

"I'm going to have dinner with my uncle later."

"Sounds boring."

A brief silence.

"Do you want to do something later tonight?"

"Like what?"

"Maybe a movie."

"I'm supposed to do something with Marlene."

"All right then." Edward suppresses his disappointment. "I guess I'll call you tomorrow."

Click.

Edward sits motionlessly on the bed, wondering if he is jealous of Marlene or not. He shouldn't be jealous because it was his own idea that David shouldn't have an exclusive relationship with Marlene so that they could have sex.

Although he is convinced that David doesn't love Marlene, he also knows that he doesn't love David, nor does David love him. *If he doesn't love David, then why should he be so insecure about their relationship?*

He shakes himself out of indolence and calls Peter, the straight Filipino guy whom he was once in love with. But all is nothing now, since he has refocused his attention on David, who may be a cow, but still a better prospect than a straight guy.

Peter is at home and he quickly agrees to see a nine-thirty show.

Having arranged his social schedule for the night, Edward sits himself before the computer and attempts to work on a short story. Minutes later, he gets bored, switches off the computer and drifts into a chaos of thoughts.

No, no, Marlene is not a threat. Marlene isn't the point at all. The point is simply that David does not give him enough security. He may see David today, but there is no guarantee that David wants to see him the next day, or the day after.

On a Saturday afternoon at two o'clock, Edward feels trapped in his apartment. He picks up the Riverside Chaucer to occupy his mind. To no avail, he closes the book and picks up the phone again. He tries calling his confidante Ellen Kim but only reaches her answering machine.

At three o'clock, Edward hops into his Honda Civic and drives off blasting the Cure's "Friday I'm in Love." The traffic is smooth all the way to San Francisco. He decides to stop at Castro to hang around and parks his car near 16th and Market.

Walking up Castro Street, he occasionally spots a white-Asian couple at whom he throws a glance of necessary disdain. He wonders why these older uglier white guys always get young Asian guys that he can't get. Then he realizes that he is dating half a white male himself.

There is nothing in the bookstore that Edward finds interesting. He spots a safer-sex poster at the bus stop and for a second he fears he may have gotten the virus from swallowing David's semen.

As he drives along the road where he used to bicycle with his cousin, he senses the oppressively impotent sanctity of the suburb—the smell of wet grass in the fogged-up air. He feels immensely liberated, realizing that he has passed eighteen. Finally out of his uncle's house.

The translucent curtains tremble at the open window of the house. His uncle opens the door in his slippers and pajamas. With his typical condescending smile, he buzzes open the gate to let Edward in. At the doorway, Edward removes his sneakers and puts them neatly on the shoe mat before stepping onto the sacred carpet.

"Are you feeling better?"

"What's better, what's worse?" asks his uncle back with a shrug. Slouching, he returns to the sofa and picks up the remote control for the TV. "How's school?"

"All right. I'm just waiting for replies from grad schools."

His uncle presses a button on the remote control. A news channel flips onto the TV screen.

"I'll go see Aunt Linda." He leaves his uncle.

The kitchen is lit with a yellowish wash from the yellow tiled walls. Stir-frying tofu and vegetables, Linda turns to him with a smile as he enters.

"How's everything, Chung Tuck?" she asks in Cantonese.

"Okay."

"Do you want anything to drink?"

"I'll help myself." Edward reaches for the refrigerator.

"There's Koala Cooler, orange juice, milk—"

"Diet Coke?"

"We haven't bought any Diet Coke since you left." Linda lets the vegetables and tofu simmer and looks at his nephew from head to toe. "You don't need Diet Coke. You're skinny as a monkey."

"Skinny? I've been working out like hell." He takes out a bottle of passion fruit and kiwi Koala Cooler and twists off the cap.

"Yeah?" she says. "Your chest seems bigger."

"I'm sorry about that night. I hope you weren't upset about me bringing David."

"Don't worry about it." With her typical forgiving smile, she asks in English, "So are you two steady?"

"Steadier than anyone I've seen before. He's also seeing a girl though. He's bisexual."

"Bisexual? Isn't it kind of dangerous?"

"Not if we practice safe sex."

Linda nods and no longer knows what to say. In the silence, Edward takes a swig of the soda in his hand. Victor enters and greets his cousin with a firm handshake. She hears Victor exchange a few brief lines with her suspicious but ultimately harmless nephew, and watches them leave the kitchen together. She stands thinking about Edward—about Edward, but about nothing in particular about Edward. The image of him lingers in her mind. She starts cooking again.

The two boys descend to the basement where the wood paneled walls are decorated with banal Americana such as a wood-framed mirror, a bad painting of Canadian winter, and a poster of the Bay Bridge. This is the room where they used to study and watch television, a space divorced from the adults who haunt the upper strata of the house.

Edward approaches the round table on which are scattered various science textbooks. Victor didn't get into Stanford or Berkeley. He ended up at San Francisco State, planning a transfer to a more prestigious institution.

Victor suggests that they go for a brief bike ride before dinner. Edward agrees. As Victor trots upstairs to tell Linda of their short outing, Edward feels a desperate urge to escape, to affirm his own world outside this house, to call up David who offers little affection.

Out of the garage, they cycle side by side on the drab suburban road. They pedal faster up the slope as the wind flutters their hair. Sporadic cars pass them. They leave their bikes on the grass surrounding the pump station and climb up the pale stony steps leading to a flat concrete plateau. Underneath their feet leaks the eerie mechanical sound of the pump station. They sit on the cold ground and watch the ghostly suburban houses.

"Are you still pissed at me about that night?"

"No."

"I'm cold." Edward sniffles his nose.

Victor does nothing but stares blankly ahead. Edward feels hopeless. Nothing that he does affects Victor. "If I'm not your cousin, would you still be my friend?"

"Of course." He looks at Edward with a childishly innocent gleam in his eyes. "Don't think that I'm hanging around with you because you're my cousin."

"I sometimes wonder about you."

Silence.

"Have you ever wanted to kiss a guy?"

"I'm straight," says Victor firmly. "I'm happy for you. I really am. David seems a nice guy."

"He thinks you're cute."

"It really irritates me when you do this, you know that?" Pause. "I know you're gay and you've proved it enough to all of us. You know what I mean? It seems that's all you ever talk about."

"It makes you uncomfortable, huh," says Edward ponderously. "Didn't you enjoy what we did?"

"It wasn't a big deal. We were just kids fooling around."

"Look, you're equally defensive about your heterosexuality as I'm about my gayness. If all of you are so comfortable about me being gay, why should you tell me not to bring David over?"

"Because he's not part of our family, that's why. *I* don't bring my girlfriend over for dinner. Dad is a stubborn and conservative man, but I respect him all the same."

"I don't."

"That's your problem."

Victor looks nervously at his watch. "Let's go."

"Why're you so cold to me after I left for college?"

"God, you can be such…"

"You literally don't even touch me anymore."

"I have a girlfriend, Edward."

Victor gets up and dusts himself. Edward follows.

"I don't mean that. All I'm saying is that you maintain a very suspicious distance from me, especially after I came out. I guess I just feel sad when I think about how close we used to be. I miss that, but I know it's impossible to be the same way we used to be because… we're different."

Victor flings his arm around Edward and tries not to imagine a virus creeping into him. He feels Edward's muscularized shoulder, which was once smaller and bonier. Victor used to see Edward as younger and weaker, so he didn't feel threatened. But now, Edward is a different creature with a menacing mind and body.

"I'm lonely, Victor."

Silence.

"David doesn't satisfy me," says Edward. "You know what I mean? Do you really love your girlfriend, Victor? Do you love her to the extent that you'll give up your career and family for her?"

"I like her a lot," says Victor without lifting his head. "She's attractive, and she's smart. We get along. We have a good time together. What more can I ask for?"

"Then I envy you. I really do."

The two cousins remain silent until they reach home. The four of them sit down to dine in the company of the television's voice. His uncle asks Victor mundane questions about school and classes, but hardly a word about Edward.

"Have you talked to your mother lately?" asks Linda.

"Yeah, last week. She seems to be doing well."

"Of course she does well. She's filthy rich," mumbles his uncle without looking at Edward. "She married the rich white man and left her son for somebody else to take care of. Your mother is a terrible mother. She's incompetent."

Despite the truth of his uncle's statements, Edward still burns with anger. But he remains tolerant. His uncle stops talking and drinks his soup. Both Linda and Victor are silent. After dinner, Edward says good-bye to his relatives and shakes hands with Victor. The gate shuts behind him. He gallops down the steps, which he can barely see in the dark.

Peter stands waiting in front of the cinema with his skinny arms crossed over his chest. Same age as Edward, Peter is boyish-looking, especially with the red baseball cap over his head. He watches Edward run to him from afar and apologize breathlessly for being late.

Inside the theater, Edward puts his feet up and scoots down to rest his head on the back of the seat. Seems like old times… only that it isn't. Edward is no longer in love with Peter, who is now seeing a Japanese American girl. They exchange a few mundane lines until the movie begins.

After the movie, Peter suggests coffee and dessert. They drive to a café where the young patrons read Nietzsche and talk about Jimmi Hendrix over cigarettes and café lattés. Peter orders a slice of cheesecake and a coffee. Edward orders a coffee with 2% milk and Equal.

Edward leans on the table and stirs his coffee like a shy girl. He then asks Peter if he can taste the cheesecake. He takes Peter's fork, cuts out a tiny corner and puts it in his mouth. He passes the fork back to Peter and watches Peter eat the cheesecake with the same fork stained with his own saliva.

Edward used to enjoy feeding Peter food when he was still in love with him, but he stopped when he found out that it was impossible to love someone who could not reciprocate. One day, Edward just stopped calling. That was three months ago. Occasionally they would see each other in social occasions where they acted nice and civil to each other.

About a month ago, Peter called Edward for some silly thing and invited him over to the new apartment. There they talked for hours. Peter kept Edward's attention by feeding him snacks: crackers, cheese and cookies that Edward could not resist. Edward renewed their friendship now filled with a dispassionate skepticism.

"I miss working out with you," says Peter.

"Have you been working out?"

"No."

"Can I have another bite?"

Peter makes a welcoming gesture and hands Edward his fork.

"I realize that if I go alone, when I see all those machines, they'll remind me of you. It will be kind of hard."

Edward is touched. He hasn't expected Peter to say that he would actually miss him.

"You know why I stopped working out with you."

"I like you a lot, as a friend," says Peter.

"But you've been fucking with my mind for the whole year. I thought you were straight at first, then I thought differently. I thought maybe you were… and I grew to like you a lot in a way that you refused to reciprocate."

"I've already told you that it's too difficult for me to turn away from what I've been constructed to be: heterosexual."

"But why did you flirt with me? You enjoyed doing that. Why did you always present yourself as sexually ambiguous with all the little insinuations? It was very painful for me when I started to like you." Edward supports his head with his hand and looks down. "Anyway."

"How's Dave?"

"He's okay." Edward sips his coffee. "How's Sherri?"

"Our relationship seems to be going pretty well."

"I'm glad." Edward feels a tinge of jealousy.

They speak very little while Edward is driving Peter home. The car glides to a stop beside the sidewalk. Peter says "See you" and leaves the car. The door slams shut. Alone in the car, Edward turns off the radio and opens his window. He breathes in some cool night air and tries not to think.

At home, there is no message on the answering machine. Edward brushes his teeth and goes to bed.

2

Feathers and Wings

During Edward's sixteenth summer, Paulina sent Edward a ticket back to Hong Kong so that he could attend her wedding with the wealthy American architect. Since she had become so foreign to him in these separated years, he didn't have any particular feelings about the matter.

So he flew back.

There was excitement, not about the wedding but rather about Hong Kong. He also went back to escape his uncle's house and its stifling petty domestic rules. He tried sleeping on the plane, but he was constantly awakened by the slightest turbulence. The plane ride was long and agitating. As the plane was landing, Edward could not wait to get out.

He felt intimidated by his sudden immersion into a sea of Chinese faces. It wasn't Chinatown. It was Hong Kong, the place where he was born, where more than five million people were like him *yet not really him*. His grandmother and her Filipino maid stood waiting among the others. She waved at the confused boy with a bulky suitcase until he spotted her with a smile of relief.

His grandmother was a woman of fifty-eight, young and stylish-looking, with a refined grace of British aristocracy. Like Paulina, she was once married to a white man who was British. From her purse, she took out a small red pocket and handed it to Edward while they were riding in the taxi.

"If you don't have enough to spend, just ask me."

"Thanks, Grandma."

"Come over to dinner some time. I hope to talk to you more now, since you're almost grown up."

"I will. Are you coming to the wedding?"

"No. Your mother didn't send me an invitation." Pause. She held Edward's still tender and soft hand. "I think about you a lot."

Edward didn't know what to say. He didn't really know what to feel or to do with her love, or any love.

The taxi dropped Edward off at Paulina's new apartment in Repulse Bay. His grandmother stayed inside the taxi until she saw a Filipino maid come down to help him with the luggage. He waved to his grandmother. She smiled back.

Dressed up, his mother was sitting on the black leather sofa with a small white man in his late thirties. Edward walked in the doorway with his suitcase. The living room and dining room were bare: some furniture and a few unopened boxes left from the moving.

The couple rose from the couch to greet Edward. The man introduced himself as John Clifford. He shook hands with Edward who offered a limp and effeminate handshake. The boy seemed young for his age, Clifford thought, as he often had a hard time in judging the age of Oriental people. He observed the immense semblance between his new wife and stepson who possessed almost the exact facial features. His skin was smooth, perhaps even smoother. He thought Edward was cute and pretty in an effeminate way.

Paulina took Edward to his room where there was a bed, a desk, a dresser and four walls. She was rather nervous, since she thought that children often hated stepfathers. She wondered if it was a mistake to have invited Edward to the wedding. She sat on the bed and watched him unpack his suitcase.

"We're going out for dinner."

"Okay."

She felt defensive, though he had not yet given her a single reason to. She tried to think positively, and suddenly she realized that she hadn't seen him for more than two years. Shouldn't he be happy to see her? Why did he act so indifferent and uninterested?

They took Edward to the Repulse Bay Hotel for dinner. The waiter seated them at a table atop which a candle burnt steadily. Edward ordered vegetable soup and a spinach salad after a brief glance at the menu.

"Are you vegetarian?" asked Clifford.

"I try to be. It's healthier and less fattening."

"Fattening?" Clifford burst out a laugh. "You shouldn't worry about that. You're so thin, and you're still a growing boy."

"You sure you'll have enough?" asked Paulina.

"Yes."

The waiter nodded with a smile, took the menus and left the family alone.

Edward sat there, drank water, ate bread and talked when he was asked to. He observed the interaction between Paulina and Clifford. They were cordial and polite toward each other. The thought of them having sex wandered into Edward's mind.

Sometimes he couldn't help looking at Clifford. He was getting excited about the fact that his mother was marrying a white man who would inject some exoticness into his life. Now he had an American stepfather.

He had wished that Clifford had been fat and ugly and mean like some nasty characters from a Dickens novel. Yes, a child torturer. It had been his guilty fantasy that this Clifford person would torture and abuse him, or perhaps even rape him.

By the end of dinner, he ended up liking Clifford more than his mother, who was artificial and utilitarian, who was always hysterically concerned about her physical appearance, who spoke such terrible English, and who acted so pretentiously feminine to please men. On the way home, he sat in the back seat of Clifford's Jaguar, staring languidly out the window.

"Edward?"

He turned to Clifford.

"Do you swim?"

"Yes. I've been taking swimming classes at school."

"I swim every other morning at the Golf Club. If you care to join me."

"That would be great."

At eleven o'clock, Edward could hardly keep his eyes open. He was lying under the blanket. In his hands was a paperback horror novel that he picked up at the airport. Just as he closed the book, about to switch off the lights, Paulina knocked on the door. She entered wearing a negligee and sat beside him on the bed.

He could smell the perfume scent of some expensive night cream on her face. Although he couldn't exactly remember what she smelt like when he was a child, he remembered that she always carried a cosmetic scent.

"You have grown so much." She smiled sheepishly. "Are you tired from the trip?"

"Yes."

Her typical redundant questions followed, to which Edward answered with little interest.

"Why do you seem so unhappy?"

"I'm fine."

"You seem to get along with John."

"He seems nice."

Silence.

"Don't make it hard for me, Chung Tuck."

"Hard for you? What did I do?"

"Just don't make it hard for me, that's all I'm saying. You act like you're so unhappy and tragic. You should be happy for me, because I'm happy with my life."

"I'm happy for you."

"Why are you angry at me?" Paulina felt more and more irritated by his nonchalance. She felt that he would do something malicious. What would he do? He would just act sulky, cold and indifferent, and perhaps utter a few nasty remarks once in a while. On top of the gossips circulating in her social circle, his unchecked tongue would be the last straw.

"I have asked you on the phone if you wanted to come back or not, haven't I? I paid for your ticket, so don't sulk and complain."

"I wanted to come back. I like Hong Kong," Edward said, "It's just that I don't care to go to your wedding. I don't like weddings. That's all."

"Do you know I love you?"

"Sure. You love me so much that you sent me away. That really showed how much you cared about me."

"I did it because I loved you. It was a great opportunity."

"Yes, a great opportunity for you to go to balls, to take afternoon naps, to get massages, to sleep with whomever you want. Of course it's great for you. You have a new husband to entertain you now."

"Bravo! Now you have feathers and wings, and you talk back at your own mother whenever you like."

"Five years, Mom. Of course my wings have grown."

She looked away and let out a frustrated sigh. He felt naked and defenseless. She could slap him, couldn't she? Wasn't that one of her favorite old tricks when he used to talk back as a child?

"Can I go to bed? I'm tired."

"If you have come back to hurt me, you're doing a good job so far," said Paulina at the doorway.

Edward felt a sudden fear within him. She would tell Clifford how mean he had treated her. Really, he hadn't done anything except for telling the truth. Silently, he watched Paulina wipe her tears with the back of her hand.

"Good night," and she was gone.

Feeling guilty and irritated, he curled up into a smaller mass under the blanket. He suddenly felt very sad, realizing that he had no home—not in Hong Kong, nor in San Francisco.

Edward woke up in his old room in the house where he grew up. He was lying naked on the bed with an erection between his thighs. Brilliant sunlight spilled from the window beside him. His flesh appeared gloriously white: no longer tanned and yellow. He touched his throbbing and sticky penis that seemed like some monster appendage on his body—something out of a David Cronenberg movie—yet it was his own. Its leaking fluid felt and smelt intimate. It felt good.

The room door opened. Paulina entered naked with her bare breasts hanging loosely. Edward lost his erection. She sat down beside him on the bed. She smiled and touched him sensually. He wanted to push her away but he felt obliged to let her touch him. Her hand moved down from his chest to his abdomen and to his penis and kept squeezing his soft and impotent organ.

"Why don't you love me?"

"I want to get a glass of water…"

He tried to get up but she secured him against the mattress with a finger on his belly button.

"Why don't you love me?"

"Because you abandoned me."

Edward curled up into a ball and felt his skin transforming. His body hair turned into feathers. A pair of bat wings grew out of his back. He turned to the window and saw his own reflection in the glass.

"Feathers and wings," said his mother in a sad voice.

"Fuck!"

Edward starts up in bed and tosses off the blanket shrouding his half-naked body. No telephone calls woke him. He has ten minutes to make it to work. His feet trample over books and crumpled pages from his paper on the postcolonial interpretation of *Jane Eyre*.

His apartment door slams shut behind him.

"Shit." He hits himself on the head and kicks the door. His keys are still inside the apartment.

The street is bright, and the air feels clean and dry. Streaks of the remaining sun's heat fall against his shoulders as he jogs along the curb. Gasping, he pulls open the glass door of Yogurt Park and slides under the counter. Ellen smiles at Edward as she is serving a young sassy girl in aerobic tights.

"I want a small… Chocolate Banana and… Peanut Butter."

Edward slips into the back room and throws on an apron. He comes back out and stands at the counter with a disoriented face. A jock approaches and asks if he can taste the Peanut Butter yogurt. With a mechanical smile, Edward takes a taster cup and fills it up with Peanut Butter frozen yogurt.

He watches the jock suck up the yogurt and glance at the pink triangle pin on Edward's apron. The jock immediately pulls his eyes away. Edward thrives on the moral superiority of his otherness.

"A small Peanut Butter."

"Any topping with that?" asks Edward with a tinge of effeminate dandyism.

"No."

"A dollar ten please."

The jock leaves without a "thank you."

The rest of the work day is hectic with faceless students in Cal sweatshirts and baseball caps flocking in and out. As their shift ends, Ellen and Edward leave together for dinner. Edward suggests Chinese food.

"I don't feel like anything too greasy," says Ellen with a whiny twang.

"How about soup and salad?"

"Okay."

She walks beside Edward with her long black hair cascading down her back. She is short and petite, full but slim. When Edward first met her in Honors English, he didn't respond to her beauty as his straight friends did. Peter had convinced Edward that she was an intensely beautiful Asian woman like a steamy heroine stepped out of the pages of a Japanese comic book.

Edward is sometimes jealous of her for the looks and attention that she gets when they both walk down the street. She can basically get anyone he desires.

Edward used to like this Korean guy who chased after her. She dismissed him so lightly: too skinny, too much acne on his face, creepy… but Edward had such a crush on him. She said that the Korean boy might have the potential to be queer, and encouraged Edward to pursue.

For a brief Thanksgiving weekend, Edward ended up sleeping with the Korean boy, who refused to kiss, refused to reciprocate after Edward gave him a blow job, refused to do anything else except lie on the bed waiting to be serviced.

After the Korean boy came, he spoke of Ellen all night long. He even admitted that he would kiss Ellen but *not* Edward because he thought that the relationship between a man and woman was sacred and spiritual.

He told Edward that Ellen wanted him to fuck her *so badly*… One night she was drunk, and she yelled at him, "Why don't you want to fuck me…" He even made Edward swear that he wouldn't tell *anyone* about what they did.

"You're afraid that I'll out you, that's all."

"Out me if you want. I don't care. What I do care is the trust between us," said the Korean boy with a cigarette between his lips and a glare in his chinky eyes. "I'd be hurt if you betrayed my trust."

When Edward entered Ellen's apartment with a face so drawn with unspoken secrets, she knew at once that they had slept together. She knew that he must have made Edward swear to secrecy and stupid shit like that.

Edward could be an intellectual, she thought, yet he was merely a child emotionally.

"See," Ellen continued her deconstruction, "he's only trying to possess your subjectivity. Swearing to secrecy? It's like high school. I can understand if you don't want to talk about it or you want to honor the trust between you boys, but you seem very disoriented and confused. It's not healthy. I worry about you."

Bit by bit Edward narrated everything to her, who immediately told him that he deserved someone better. He sighed and agreed, but he couldn't take his mind off the Korean boy. He said that it might not be the best thing, but it was all he had at the moment.

A week later, Edward woke up and told the Korean boy off.

At Café Intermezzo, they each order a green salad with poppy seed dressing and sit facing each other by the window. Edward tears a small corner from his bread and stuffs it in his mouth. He looks out the window, into the darkened street, where homeless men and women gather and students pass them nonchalantly.

"They want you to moderate a panel on film and video at the Asian American Arts Conference," says Ellen with a forkful of salad. "Would you be interested?"

"Sure." With a blank face, he plunges his fork into a slice of tomato, raises it to mid-air and decides not to eat it. "I'm not hungry."

"You're so crazy. You're anorexic. Honestly, you're like really skinny, and I think you should eat more. It's not good for your body if you're too thin."

"I'm fine." Edward takes a sip of Diet Coke.

"Are you seeing Dave tonight?"

"He hasn't called." A beat. "He was supposed to call before I left for work. I was so depressed waiting so I went to sleep. I woke up at three twenty and he still hasn't called. I ran out of the apartment for work, and realized that I left my keys in the apartment. I'm in such a mess."

"Look, Edward, he isn't worth it. He's an asshole if he doesn't call you when he says he will. It's as simple as that."

"I don't think I love him. I guess I like him, but I don't understand why I think about him so much."

"He's mediocre. You deserve someone better."

"Why am I always stuck with mediocre people who don't even give a shit about me?"

"Because you give them too much power." Ellen pierces the cherry tomato with her fork. "You're like my sister who always needs a man. She is someone of high caliber, but she always gets stuck with mediocre men. It's desperation. You have to get yourself out of the old system. It's not Dave, and it's not Peter. It's the way you are. You always need someone, so you just grab whoever you can and put him into this obsessive role in your life."

"Yeah," Edward looks at his salad. "He's one of the better guys I've been with. It's the most substantial relationship I've had so far. He is reciprocative, at least in bed. But sometimes, little things bother me."

"You're just like me." She lights a cigarette. "I need a lot of attention too, but I hide it well. Sometimes I'd go crazy when I expected to talk to Kenny but I couldn't reach him. You just have to occupy your mind with something else."

"Like what?"

"Like things that are more important." Ellen takes a puff and rests the cigarette on the ashtray. "You know these are just very petty things. Everyone has to deal with them. You shouldn't let them deprive you of your energy because you have so much to do. Your academic work. Your creative work. Your career. You know what I mean? It's just not worth it."

"School's as much a game as anything else… like who really cares about stupid deconstruction and postcolonial shit."

"What is real to you then?"

"My writing."

"Then write. Fuck Dave."

"But I can't when I'm so emotionally dependent on someone. I just can't think about anything else but him when I don't hear from him. All I can do is go to sleep and hope that I will be awakened by a phone call."

At ten o'clock they return to Ellen's apartment because Edward is too depressed to go home. He fears that there are no messages on his answering machine. As soon as he enters Ellen's apartment, he grabs her phone and calls home.

"Did he call?" She sips from a glass of ice coffee in her hand.

"Yeah." With a smile, he hangs up and dials David's number. David picks up the phone and asks him if he would like to come over. Edward says, "Sure."

As soon as Edward gets off the phone, he bounces off the bed and strides into Ellen's kitchen for snacks. Ellen opens the door to the balcony and takes out her pack of Marlboros. She sits by the edge of the door and lights a cigarette. Edward returns with a caramel rice cake in his hand. His face is boyish and gay. The artificial caramel melts in his mouth. She hands him her glass of ice coffee from which he takes a few sips.

"So you're seeing Dave later?"

"Yeah." With a musing look, he brushes back the fringes of hair over his forehead and sits with his hands over his bent knees. "I'll go over to his place around midnight."

For the rest of the evening, he spends his time watching TV and half-studying with Ellen. Neither of them gets any work done. They chat. David's name comes up every three minutes of their conversation. Edward does not seem to realize how obsessive he is while Ellen thinks the whole thing is trivial. Within a few months, she predicts, David would drift out of his life just like the rest of the other insignificant sexually ambiguous guys. She tries reading, but she can't help talking to him.

She likes Edward because he has a sense of nonchalance toward academia, unlike her other nerdy intellectual English majors, Peter being one of them, who take themselves so damn seriously. Absolutely uninvolved in the petty race of academia, Edward just seems to breeze past his academic work with decent grades. She admires his creative side which prevents him from being too bogged down by theory and criticism. People who play the game well go on to graduate school. Others, too exhausted and bored, venture into the world of petty mundane things.

"I'm really bored." Ellen flops on the bed with her long black hair spreading over the sheets. "I think I have to stay here for another year."

"You can relax for another year and not worry about grad school."

"But I'm getting burnt out. Everyone is so boring and bourgeois. I'm really happy for you, since you'll be going away for what you want to do. Where're you applying?"

"UCLA, USC and NYU for film. Then Yale and Berkeley for English. It's going to be stressful waiting for replies."

"If you get into Berkeley, would you stay?"

"No," Edward says firmly. "Unless I don't get into anywhere else."

"I think I'm going to break up with Kenny." Silence. "He's dorky, boring and petty. It's pettiness that I can't stand, you know what I mean? I don't understand why these Asian guys are so petty."

She sits up with angst. "He's so competitive. We got back the paper from Romanticism. He told me he got an A minus, and I congratulated him. Then he asked me what I got. I told him I got an A. He just didn't say another word. Not even the slightest encouragement. God, I couldn't stand his stupid sulky face and his shifty eyes. So what? Can't he admit that I can do as well as he does, or even better?"

"Men are petty." Edward looks at his watch: ten more minutes to midnight.

"I'm through with these petty bourgeois kids. I want someone older and rich. Someone who's not as consuming. I'll just spend my weekends with him, and we'll go on trips. I can drop him if I want. He wouldn't care, because he has money and he can find another replacement whenever he wants."

Edward wants exactly the contrary—a consuming relationship that will engage him day and night. Something destructive and passionate. Some guy around his age who is devoted and suicidal. *David doesn't have enough passion.* He hates to think how cold David could be. His silence, his occasional sarcastic remarks, his nonchalance. He wants David to drag him into an abyss.

But he is the one who is in the abyss. When he looks up, he sees David standing up there looking down nonchalantly at him.

In the same summer that his mother got remarried, Edward reconnected with his childhood friend Lee Man Wai, who had grown to be a tall and attractive Chinese boy. Although their friendship had been intense when they were children, it seemed to be devoid of sexuality. Man Wai did not seem to have changed except in his physicality, still effeminate and extremely innocent.

On the other hand, Edward's own sexuality constantly threatened to burst out of his skin. All these young guys he saw on the street, on the tram, in shopping malls… he stole their images at first sight. Then every night, he masturbated to them. It was a routine.

On a typical hot and humid summer afternoon, Man Wai and Edward went to the cinema. They both had a passion for horror movies. The empty air-conditioned auditorium was a relief to the irritable heat outside. They sat down and hung their feet on the back of the seats before them. The floor was covered with paper bags, spilt soda, popcorn, dried squid and other trash. His ear had readjusted to processing Cantonese as the normal language: his mother tongue, which had turned foreign, was once again familiar.

The two boys shared a paper-bagful of sweet popcorn between them, and became suddenly self-conscious of their existence and abnormalities. For Edward, it was his undefined homosexuality and his experience in the West: the fact that he was a Hong Kong boy drenched in salt water. For

Man Wai, his feeling of abnormality was more blurry. His Catholicism, his parents, his effeminacy all blended into confusion. They wanted to speak their hearts out, yet they feared each other's normality.

It started to rain heavily when they got out of the movie. Without an umbrella, they remained under an awning for a few minutes with other passersby. They ran out of patience shortly and dashed into a restaurant on the other side of the street. The chill-conditioned air made them shiver. They sat at a table and ordered fruit punches. Man Wai was hungry, so he ordered a plate of spaghetti.

The rain had stopped. They were sitting beside a large glass window. Edward touched the vaporized surface of the glass and wrote the English word "Crazy" with his finger. Man Wai looked at the word on the glass. It was soon covered by a film of vapor. Man Wai looked down at his half finished spaghetti and no longer felt the desire to eat forever. He wished he had the determination to starve himself to death.

"Are you all right?"

"Yeah," said Man Wai. "I'm glad you're so happy all the time."

"*I'm* happy all the time?"

"You're always happy, even when we were in school together."

"You just don't know how lonely I feel all the time. I mean, I smile. I joke. I act like I'm happy outside but I'm not really…"

"How's your mother?"

"She's getting married with that American man. I don't really care. She does what she wants, and I do what I want."

"You're happier."

Silence. Edward was irritated. He felt inferior because Man Wai didn't see him as his equal. He was happier? A sense of alienation swept him. They were strangers after all.

"There were days when I was in class, I looked at the window and really felt like jumping out. I didn't want to care anymore," said Man Wai. "But I didn't do it because I thought of my parents."

Silence.

"Maybe I'll kill myself after they die. My father is almost sixty." Man Wai sipped his fruit punch. "I don't want to live a life that I don't want to live. I'm doing everything for everyone else."

"So what do you want?"

"I don't know."

After their afternoon snack, the two boys parted, each taking a taxi in separate directions.

The taxi driver was playing some Cantonese opera in the car. Edward felt the music unbearably jarring, but he was too exhausted to protest. His mind was heavy. The taxi driver stopped at a traffic light where a crowd of people crossed the street: young and thin students in their uniforms and thick glasses, professional men and women in suits, old people with red plastic bags... There were so many people, and he felt insignificant. He could have been any one of them, and vice versa. What right did he have to claim abnormality and monstrosity? Was he not the same as everybody else?

The taxi stopped beside his grandmother's apartment building. He paid the driver and stepped onto the wet sidewalk covered with animal blood from the meat market. He passed by a newspaper stand and glanced through the magazines and newspapers. He left when the old man insistently tried to sell Edward a newspaper.

The Filipino maid greeted Edward with a smile and opened the gate. His grandmother was sitting on the couch with a silk scarf around her neck. She put down her knitting needles. Her face lit up as she saw her grandson.

"Tea?" asked his grandmother.

"Sure."

The maid returned with two cups of milk tea. His grandmother stirred her cup and took a sip. She asked if the boy wanted a mango, a banana, or an apple. Edward politely replied that he was full.

He was silent but comfortable with the warm tea in his hand. Their eyes met. She smiled at him and he shyly smiled back.

"I'm knitting a sweater for you," said his grandmother. "When it's done, I'll send it to your uncle's house."

"Thanks."

"You're older now, and I don't see you very often. There are things I want to talk to you about."

Already drained by the last few hours spent with Man Wai, he tried to be attentive. He wanted to stop thinking about Man Wai.

"Is your uncle treating you well?"

"Yes, Grandma, don't worry about me." He didn't want to open the can of worms.

She nodded, finished the last sip of her tea and put the cup aside.

"I think it's good for you to be in America. Hong Kong is no stable home for young people. Your mother was right in sending you to school. I wish I could see you more often. I don't want you to worry about me. I want you to do what you want and go wherever you want."

He nodded, and felt old.

"Your father married too young. To tell you the truth, Edward, I didn't approve of their marriage. Because your father wanted, what could I have said? I just hope he was happy."

Silence. He took a banana from the fruit bowl and peeled off its yellow skin. He sank his teeth into the ivory phallus.

"Edward, promise to call me if you need anything, I'll do my best."

Edward nodded.

"I'm old and perhaps conservative, but I've gone through a lot too. Some day, I'll tell you things that have happened to me. Things you could never imagine."

It was six thirty. He had promised to meet Clifford and his mother for dinner at seven. He wanted to stay, but he had to leave. He felt closer to his grandmother. They parted at the doorway. She asked him to call her. At least see her once more. Just as he was to step out, he kissed her on the cheek.

Edward did not usually kiss. Not his mother. Not his dead father's cheek. Not anyone else. But this kiss was out of a spontaneous desire, out of something common within the both of them.

"Are you horny?"

"Are you?"

"I asked you first."

"Maybe."

"It's late though. I have work tomorrow."

"Are you ashamed of me?"

"What do you mean?"

"I mean when you're always so distant to me in front of your friends."

"Do I seem distant to you?"

"It kind of makes me feel uncomfortable. I didn't know your friends, and you invited me over. I just sat there, you know, and I didn't know if I should talk to you or talk to all these strangers. Do you know what I mean?" Edward sniffles his runny nose and pulls the blanket further up to his chin. He turns away from David.

"I'm sorry," says David. "It's not the first time I've done something like that."

"No."

"I have this problem with the people that I was close to. Lina told me the same thing when we went out in high school," says David quietly.

Their bodies are frozen, in the warmth, under one blanket, their backs facing each other's.

"If you don't deal with your problems, Dave, they'll always be there."

"I'm lazy." This is an honest statement, but what does honesty amount to if it is so unproductive.

"Just don't do it to me next time."

"I'm sorry."

A murmur in the dark. The sound of a runny nose. The ruffling of sheets. Silence. A snore. Breathing. What more can he say? Edward's eyes are still closed, but his mind is so brimmed with discontent that he cannot fall asleep.

He thinks of getting out of his lover's bed and going home. Leaving this compromising comfort, marginal pleasure. He wishes he had the strength.

A hand touches his lap. So full of sex that Edward cannot resist but give in. But he remains still and lets the hand incite him. He is sick of calling, making plans and being the demanding one. David nudges closer. Edward feels the warm breaths upon the nape of his neck. He is forgetting that just a few minutes ago he was so close to walking out. He turns and kisses David deeply.

"Do you want to fuck me?" asks David.

"You mean anal sex?"

"Yeah. We haven't done it for a while."

David goes down on Edward, pulls down Edward's underwear, and puts his mouth around Edward's cock.

"Lie on your back," says David.

Edward complies and lies supine on the bed as Edward continues to suck him.

"Does it feel good?"

Edward lifts his head and sees David pulling off his briefs. He watches David kneel on top of Edward and spits on his hand.

"What are you doing?"

"Just relax."

"But shouldn't we use…"

"I trust you."

David smears his spit on Edward's cock and slowly sits on it. Edward feels a little awkward as David tries to aim his cock.

"Aw…"

"Wait…"

"Okay… it's going in."

Edward can hear the pouding of his heart. It's his first time fucking someone without a condom.

"You like it?"

Edward holds onto David's sides as David moves up and down. Edward digs his thumbs into David's lean abdomen.

"Feels good, doesn't it?" asks David.

"Yeah."

Edward wakes up beside David. The first thing he remembers is that David let Edward come inside him and told Edward to stay inside. They slept attached for a while. Now he is still sleeping beside Edward like a little hairless animal.

The alarm clock breaks the silence with the annoying voice of some DJ babbling about castration and other psycho-babble. David springs up from the bed like a Chinese zombie and turns off the alarm. He collapses back onto the bed and pulls the comforter over his head. Edward lies awake with his naked body. He doesn't have to go to work, and ironically he is the one who wants to get out of bed.

A few more minutes pass. The alarm clock sounds again. David springs up once more and turns it off. He falls back against the bed and stretches.

"Good morning, Edward."

Edward smiles. David kisses him deeply on the lips and proceeds toward his hardness.

They take a shower together and walk to the BART station. On the way, they grab two muffins, one each, and a cup of coffee, with Equal and a lot of cream, which they share. They sit on a bench next to the BART station. David finishes his muffin first and glances at his watch. Edward sips the coffee and passes the cup to David. He realizes that in the next five minutes David will be gone.

Five minutes later, Edward is walking home alone.

In the morning chill, pigeons are pecking on the ground. Homeless people lean against glass storefronts. He glances at his own reflection as he walks by a store window. Why does he feel so dependent, so weak and so miserable? In less than nine months, he will be leaving Berkeley for somewhere new, somewhere he can be reborn.

No, he won't stay in Berkeley even if he gets in. He will go to film school and focus on his art. Fuck them all, he says to himself. Fuck David. Fuck everyone. Yet these impulsive proclamations evaporate after a few seconds of passion.

He will still wait for his phone calls.

Edward realizes that sometimes it may not be the place or the time. The misery is in himself. The monstrosity. The hole in his heart. No one can fix it. It wouldn't be David. It wouldn't be Victor. It wouldn't be any one else. He must curb his appetite in order not to let himself be devoured from within.

And sometimes, David does melt his heart, and it's enough to forget everything else at the moment.

Edward woke up on the plane. His eyes felt sore. It was probably from all the sobbing. For a second, he couldn't tell if it was night or day. He looked out of the airplane window and saw the bright clouds. The stewardess was serving breakfast. The man beside him ate everything while Edward only ate the fruit.

He no longer felt sad when the plane landed. He was scared, because he could hardly speak English. His senses had to be awake and sharp. The stewardess announced something about "landing." The safety belt sign came on, and he checked his safety belt.

A travel escort, who had a Chinese face but spoke only English, came up to his seat after the landing. The woman escorted the boy in getting his baggage, and then out of immigration and customs. The immigration officer, a black woman, was kind enough not to harass the Chinese boy who could scarcely speak English. He tried his best. Careful not to make grammatical mistakes.

His uncle, whom Edward had met once when he came to Hong Kong, was waiting outside with his hands in his ski jacket pockets. He waved to the boy and went up to greet him. The escort left after a cordial smile.

Edward pushed the cart of luggage outside and waited for his uncle to drive the car around. It was an August day. The weather was foreign to Edward. Dry and cool, unlike Hong Kong's, which was wet and hot.

His uncle was kind enough to help Edward carry the suitcases inside the house, his new home. A nice house, Edward thought. The first rule that his uncle informed him was to take off his shoes before stepping onto the carpet. The living room was bright. There was a scent of freshness unlike anything that he had smelt before. Something new and exotic.

"Chung Tuck," said a female voice.

He turned around and saw a middle-aged woman with a full face and a gentle smile beside a slim younger boy. She was wearing an apron. She shook hands with Edward. The younger boy said "hi" with a smile.

The two boys got acquainted quickly. Victor was kind to him. They frolicked in the garden, played video games, and watched television together. It was only natural that they grew close in such a culturally claustrophobic house. Victor had no peer to play with since his parents were highly selective about the friends he made. His father forbade him to play with the neighborhood kids who cussed and rode skateboards. Before Edward, Victor's only source of companionship was from his mother and father. Now another boy was here, and everything was different.

Linda liked the new boy, who was often eager to help with housework. He also took away some pressure from her as she didn't have to babysit Victor twenty-four hours a day. On the contrary, his uncle held a silent suspicion. He observed Edward whenever he had a chance. He had a rather low opinion of Edward's mother—a social butterfly, a fickle and bitchy woman whom he would not otherwise deal with if she had not been his sister. Her offspring must carry some of her blood, since he so resembled his mother. He was a cute boy, and would probably grow into a handsome youth. He appeared to be nice, obedient and sweet so far, but there was no guarantee what he would become in a year or two. His uncle was skeptical. Not that he was particularly skeptical toward the boy, he was simply skeptical about life. Or so he justified his prejudice.

A month had passed. His aunt was sitting on the bed with her reading glasses and a Jackie Collins novel. On the night table lay another book, a Chinese literary novel, *The Dreams of the Red Chamber*. She switched from one book to another at her whims. His uncle opened the door a small gap and went to bed. Linda put away the book and turned to her husband. She reached to touch his unresponsive body.

"Do you think we did the right thing?"

"Where else could he be?"

"In a boarding school."

"Chung Tuck has been very good, and I think it's also good for Victor to have some companionship. They seem to be getting along."

"She should have sent him to a boarding school, but she insisted that the boy stay with us."

"Look, Daddy, you're just doing your sister a favor. She pays for everything that the boy needs."

"Still…"

"I don't understand you. We've discussed this before and you agreed to take the boy in. You can't turn back on your words now. And I don't see why this is such a big deal. Your sister offered to pay you rent, but you refused to accept it."

"It's not the money," said the man with a sigh.

"Then what is it?"

"I hope he isn't a bad influence."

"My God, Daddy," Linda burst out in English. "Give that boy a break. You're always so quick to judge people. Look, he's just a kid, and a kid can't be bad."

In the other room, Edward and Victor lay under separate blankets, on separate beds no more than three feet apart. The room door was open a crack and they could vaguely hear the adults talking. Edward heard his name come up, but did know what they were talking about. He shifted uneasily under the blanket. If his uncle and aunt did not want him, where would he go? Would they send him back to Hong Kong?

"Can we close the door?" whispered Edward.

"No, let's leave it open," whispered Victor back in the clumsy Cantonese of an ABC (American Born Chinese).

"You don't have to be afraid of the dark anymore, I'm here."

"Yeah, but Daddy said we should keep the door open."

"All right."

"Do you miss your mother?"

"No," said Edward, and reproduced a phrase from some American movie, "She don't love me."

The younger boy didn't know what to say. After Victor fell asleep, Edward was still awake. He shifted back and forth in bed. He couldn't get to sleep. Some time passed. The darkness made him feel weary. The warmth of the bed was becoming stifling and uncomfortable.

His feet touched the carpet. His eyes could see quite a lot in the dark, like a cat's eyes. He made his way through the doorway into the living room as a cool draft assaulted him. He huddled on a chair with arms over his knees in the kitchen. The only illuminating sources were the moonlight from the window and the glowing digital configurations on the microwave oven. His nose was getting clogged up.

It wasn't the first time he felt lonely. It was the first time he felt completely alone. Man Wai was thousands of miles away.

"Chung Tuck?"

His aunt startled him. He didn't know what to say. Even this moment of privacy was intruded.

"Are you all right?"

She approached the boy who sniffled back the watery stuff in his nose. He could scarcely utter, "I'm thirsty, so I came to get a glass of water."

"Me too."

Linda was wearing a pale nightgown with a material that glimmered under the moonlight. This woman was not his mother, because she was a *real* mother. She had the kind of overflowing benevolence that his mother could never have. Someone who really cared for her son. His mother was different. She was too beautiful and too proud to be motherly.

A stream of silver flowed from the tap. His aunt handed him a glass of water. He looked at the glass of water, whose clarity and transparency absorbed him for a second.

She watched the boy drain the water. She wanted to hold him but feared that it might make him weak. She knew if he fell into her arms he would cry and sob. She would do it for her own son, so why not *this* boy?

"Good night, Aunt Linda," said the boy and stepped out of the kitchen.

She watched the boy's shape disappear into darkness. She took a sip of water. She was no longer thirsty. Why didn't she hug him? She should have done it. All that mattered, really, was the boy's temporary relief. How many times had she felt so alone and wanted someone to hug her but no one was there?

Edward remembers that first night in his uncle's kitchen. Alone again, Edward is sitting beside the glass door to the balcony in his apartment. Moonlight spills through the glass onto his face.

He can't fall asleep.

The glass of water lies on the table two feet from his arm. He reaches out and takes a sip. He isn't thirsty, but it feels good to drink, to feel the coolness down his throat.

David Wong. The name floats up in his mind.

Nothing has changed.

David is not spending the night with him. Big deal. This is not the first time Edward is alone. Why should he feel anything different? *This too too sullied flesh should melt and dissolve itself into a dew.* The line from *Hamlet* drifts into his mind. In the morning his loneliness will evaporate. He will be occupied by errands, classes and work.

Edward lets out a groan and covers his face. When he can objectively see his lonely self, he feels less alone. He goes back to bed and closes his eyes. Tomorrow he will see David. Probably.

What wakes Edward is not the alarm clock but knocks from the door. Cold air pricks the skin on his half naked body. Knocks again. His cousin is standing outside with his hands in his pockets.

Edward opens the door.

"Hi," says Victor. "Can I talk to you?"

They sit facing each other, Edward on his bed and Victor on a chair at a corner of the room. Edward pulls up the blanket to cover his body.

"I'm sorry to wake you."

"Did you break up?"

"Well… I don't know. I mean… it's more me."

"Why?"

"What is wrong with me?" Victor runs his fingers through his hair and turns away from Edward.

"I don't know."

"I think I'm bisexual."

"So what's the problem?"

"I don't know."

"Have you told her?"

"No."

"Why're you confessing this to me?"

Silence.

"I thought you'd understand."

"I don't know what to say." Edward sits up more. "What do you want me to say? You know I'm always on your side, but I'm not that better off than you are. I can't tell you what you are, because in the end you'll have to figure it out yourself."

Edward gets up from the bed and gives his cousin a glass of orange juice. He watches the younger boy drink it indolently. For a few seconds, an old passion rises within him.

Linda and his uncle went to Reno alone one weekend in early December. They had intended to bring the teenagers along, but they realized neither of them was extremely enthusiastic and so they took the opportunity to steal away. In the children's absence, they spent their time in casinos.

Victor was fifteen, and Edward was seventeen. That weekend, Edward was busy polishing up his applications for college. The deadline that he had set for himself was Monday. On Friday evening, he sat for hours in the room using Victor's computer, going through the final drafts of his application essays.

In the kitchen, Victor was cooking dinner. He boiled some spaghetti and opened a can of tomato sauce. He felt slightly inadequate, since he only knew how to cook canned food. While he was waiting for the spaghetti to cook, he stole a cookie every now and then, watching television. He left the kitchen to check on Edward, who was still sitting absorbed before the computer screen.

For a moment he stood at the doorway but said nothing. He observed the older boy with a fascination. He felt a sudden pleasure as a voyeur spying on someone whom he had spent so much time with. It was the first time he saw his cousin by himself. There was some unacknowledged beauty in the gaze.

"Are you hungry yet?"

"Kind of." Edward got up from the computer. "Do you need to use the computer?"

"No."

They ate facing each other in the company of the television voice. Victor started playing with his spaghetti after a few forkfuls. Edward ate silently with his dazed eyes staring at some blank space.

"Do you want to see a movie or something?"

"Huh?"

"Do you want to see a movie?"

"I don't know. I should work on my applications."

"You already finished them two weeks ago. I'm bored, man."

"What do you want to see?"

Edward always gave in. Victor felt his power over him. When they grew up together, Victor often played the leader even though Edward was the older one. He realized that Edward was dependent on him. Edward would simply follow if he suggested a place to go. He was more popular than Edward in school. He was in an elitist clique, while Edward had friends who were neither popular nor rich. In fact, Edward had no close friends but Victor.

The two boys went out to catch the nine o'clock show. Edward bought a pack of Twizzlers. The movie began. Some sort of a routine Hollywood thriller. There was sex, heterosexual sex, to which each of the boys reacted silently and separately within themselves.

They drove home. It was almost midnight.

Edward was too tired to work on his applications. He stood staring at the computer screen for a minute, and saved the files which he had been working on.

"Are you going to sleep?" Victor was standing barefoot on the carpet.

"Yeah." Edward switched off the computer.

In the room where the two boys had been living together, Edward took off his T-shirt and jeans. His socks were rolled into two small balls lying on the carpet under his bed.

They were each sleeping on a separate bed. Victor felt something different and new after watching the movie that night. The image of bodies gyrating against each other… Then he heard occasional sighs from the bed next to his.

"Edward?"

"Huh?"

"Something wrong?"

"I can't sleep."

"Why?"

"I don't think I'll get into any of the schools."

"Don't be stupid. You do so well in school."

Silence.

"Do you want me to sleep over?"

"Yeah," said Edward softly.

Their bodies had grown, and the bed seemed smaller for the two boys to sleep on, but they managed to fit without a foot or a hand dangling over the edges.

"Are you all right?"

"Sometimes I don't know what I want to do," said Edward in the dark.

"I just don't see there is anything at all I should hope for."

Victor gently patted his older cousin. His hand touched the soft skin of the seventeen-year-old boy. The feeling was nice. His skin was smooth. Edward could easily have been a girl, thought Victor even though he had never touched a girl's body before. His cousin's body seemed to match all the descriptions of a girl's body except for certain anatomical parts.

Edward woke up and dashed into the bathroom. He closed the door, stood before the toilet and pulled down his briefs. His penis was sticking straight out in an angle. Within a second, white stuff leaked awkwardly out of the tip. Gobs of it fell into the toilet bowl. Relieved, Edward flushed the toilet and went back to bed. He glanced at the digital clock which read 7:23 AM. He glided back under the blanket beside his sleeping cousin's body.

"What time is it?"

"Go back to sleep."

"Your feet... cold."

"I'm sorry."

Silence. Victor was asleep. Edward shut his eyes but could not fall asleep.

The water glass is empty. Victor is still sitting in Edward's apartment. Time is slipping by. Edward is already late for a class.

"Do you have class today?"

"Yeah, I should be in school now." Victor raises his melancholic gaze from the void to Edward. "Am I taking your time?"

"It's okay. I don't get to see you that much anyway."

Edward examines his cousin and tries to understand what attractiveness he finds in him. He is sick of that spell Victor had cast over him.

In their mutual silence, he realizes that Victor is here for both a consolation and a proof of superiority. He thinks that Victor knows all along. It's only that the he doesn't want to admit it. By not admitting his queerness, Victor can constantly use Edward's image to play off his straightness.

It's three o'clock in the afternoon. Edward watches his friends Peter and Ellen scribbling on their notebooks, and realizes that he is in fact in a lecture hall. He stops spinning his pen and starts scribbling down the fragments he hears:

Cultural Territorialism

Homi Bhabha

cultural migrancy

African American

Deconstruction

Spike Lee

editing

The time has come. The professor stops speaking. Students scribble down the last sentences and flock to the professor for paper extensions. Edward rises from his chair and waits for the slow traffic swarming out of the lecture hall.

This is his last year at Berkeley. Edward wonders if he is really so excited and eager to leave. What if he doesn't get into grad school? What will he do? He isn't an American resident, though he is rather culturally American, or perhaps Asian American. Does he want to go back to Hong Kong? No, he has already told his grandmother. He doesn't want to go back to Hong Kong.

"Shall we go for coffee?" suggests Peter.

"Sure," says Ellen.

"Café Milano, Edward?"

In Café Milano, the three Asians are chinkily eyeing for an open table. Ellen insists on sitting in the smoking section, so they go upstairs where Tommy is sitting with two gothic fag hags.

"Edward!" screams Tommy.

With a smile, Edward approaches Tommy. They kiss each other on the lips. Not that Edward has anything against kissing, he simply dislikes the salivariness on Tommy's lips. Skinny and faggy, Tommy is a Jewish boy from New York, the queerest freshman and probably the queerest fag on campus. Tommy wears a leather jacket plastered with *ACT-UP* and *QUEER NATION* stickers, army boots and a *READ MY LIPS* T-shirt.

"So how's Dave?"

"He's all right."

"Is he still dating Marlene?"

"I guess so."

"David Wong is a slut," snorts Tommy and sips the foam off his mocha. "But he's cute anyway. Do you mind if I sleep with him?"

"It's up to him," says Edward matter-of-factly.

"Cool, I'll ask him."

Edward returns to his Asian American friends who have already bought themselves coffee. Tommy continues to gossip and scam with his girl friends. Peter tears a corner from the chocolate croissant and stuffs the glittery dough into his mouth.

"May I have a bite?" ask Ellen and Edward in unison.

Both Ellen and Edward take a bite off the chocolate croissant. Muttering an "mmm," Ellen savors the baked dough in her mouth. Peter finishes the croissant in a few more bites and sips his mocha. Ellen and Edward constantly accuse each other of being anorexic, of not eating enough, of being skinny. This drama of competitive anorexia is often amusing to Peter who sees the whole complex as a "girlish thing."

What about that straight and homophobic *Daily Cal* columnist Hung, whom Peter went jogging with in the middle of the night during their freshman year? Now in his senior year, Hung has given up the project of losing weight. He realizes that it isn't his appearance that needs change, but rather, it is the objective notion of aesthetics.

In his column, Hung violently attacks mainstream "white" aesthetics and takes on the self-appointed role to represent all Asian males in America. He points a militant finger at the Asian women who date white men and accuses them of being "whitewashed." Little does Hung know, his best friend Peter and that obnoxious faggot Edward have cracked a million jokes behind his back. The truth is… it isn't quite a political reason that Hung can't get his girl. It's simply that Hung is physically repulsive, mentally idiotic and talentlessly arrogant.

"Is that the infamous Tommy?" asks Peter.

"Yeap," says Edward.

"He's kind of scary looking," says Peter.

"But he's very political, and he practically knows every gay person on campus. He was a close friend of mine when I first came out. We used to hang out a lot."

Ellen steals a glance at Tommy. Tommy is talking animatedly with his hands and wrists flying liberally in the air. Ellen refocuses her gaze back on her friends. She wonders if she would still be so close to Edward if he weren't queer.

"I want to be more political," says Edward, "but somehow I just lost the passion. I guess I was more political when I first came out. I wore gay T-shirts to classes and I went to a few protests. But I got tired of it, you know what I mean? I never like protests anyway. I just don't see how much

I can accomplish by participating in a protest."

"You have a point," says Peter, with a dramatic pause and a sip of mocha, "I believe I can be more productive if I'm not going to a demonstration. It isn't the only way to help the community."

"Yet I believe public protests are important."

"I agree, but I think some people are more fitted to one form of protests, like marching in front of the White House or going on a hunger strike while other people are more fitted to other kinds of—"

"Fuck you, Peter," Ellen snorts. "You're such a snobby little elitist. All you want to say is that you're an intellectual and your intellectual work *is* your protest and your contribution to the community."

"I mean, yeah," says Peter, blushing, "we're not all the same. Some people are more privileged than others. I go to demonstrations, but I still think I can utilize my time in something else that could be more radically productive."

"For me, I don't think it's really a matter of productivity," says Edward. "When I'm at a protest, I just don't feel that I'm all for the cause. I always have doubts and certain things that I don't agree with completely. A protest forces me to take a side... which is kind of uncomfortable because I feel hypocritical if I'm doing it only half-heartedly without a complete affirmative belief."

"Well," says Ellen, "but don't you think that we always have to take a side which is more politically correct even if we don't completely agree with all the issues. There will always be some degree of disagreement, but because of the immediacy and violence of an oppressive situation we are forced to react now. We sometimes just don't have the luxury to sit back and contemplate on the issues too much."

"Yeah," Edward vaguely agrees.

3

Undress

It was the first time Edward tasted semen. On the second night of that weekend when his parents were at Reno, Victor touched Edward's body beginning from the smooth curve between his neck and shoulder… He was trying to imagine if there could be a difference between Edward's and a girl's. Edward cracked up and said he was ticklish. He reached out to touch Victor's thighs, brushing by the erection under the garment. When the laughter and giggling faded, silence poured in with a flood of compulsive pleasure.

They didn't quite know what they were doing. Their bodies crushed against the other, their erect penises nestling in the enclosed space between their flesh. Not long, they were holding onto each other's penises and jerking them.

"Can I put it in your mouth?"

Edward looked at Victor and closed his mouth around Victor's penis. Edward didn't know exactly what to do… but he wanted to please.

"Do you like it?"

"Maybe a little faster."

Edward complied. He felt Victor was more and more responsive. Victor watched Edward suck him in silent pleasure. Suddenly, he touched Edward's face and pulled his penis out Edward's mouth.

"You don't like it?" asked Edward.

"No, I'm getting there."

Edward looked at Victor's beautiful penis glistening with his saliva.

"You want me to do you?" asked Victor.

"No." Edward put Victor's penis back in his mouth.

Victor saw Edward's eagerness to please him. It didn't take him long to get close again. Later, he watched Edward gently let his penis slip out after he came and swallow after a moment of hesitation.

"Are you okay?" asked Victor.

"Yeah." Edward smiled.

The telephone rang, startling them. Victor hesitantly picked up the phone by the bed.

"Hello?"

"Victor?"

"Yeah." His mother's voice startled him. He stood naked with his still hard penis and talked to his parents as Edward lay on the bed beside him. They both felt a little guilty.

Later that night, they slept separately.

Beep.

Beep.

"It's Ellen, just calling to see what's up—"

Beep.

"Hey, it's Victor. Give me a call, man."

Beep.

Edward stops the answering machine and turns to David who already has his arms around Edward's midriff. They kiss. Once. A short one. Then they kiss more. David always closes his eyes to focus on the sensation while Edward always keeps his eyes open.

Edward likes to watch David when he closes his eyes during kissing. That immense amount of romanticization that David invested into sensations amuses Edward. On the contrary, Edward is an intensely visual person, so he watches.

After sex, they are sprawling in bed, close to each other. David sniffles. Edward pulls the blanket to cover their naked bodies. David kisses Edward. It's a desexualized kiss: one that is more affectionate than lustful.

"My cousin has been calling me a lot," says Edward.

"He probably needs support."

"But I'm kind of tired of it. If I've liberated myself from the closet, why should I have to carry someone else's burden? He just wants to talk to me, to fill me up with silence, and I'll just feel more frustrated and claustrophobic when I see his parents next time."

"He's your cousin."

They are holding each other in a somewhat awkward position, yet the warmth and staticity is too comfortable to be disrupted.

"I may go back to Hong Kong during Christmas," says Edward.

"That sounds fun."

"What are you doing?"

"Nothing much. I'll probably spend Christmas with my parents."

Silence. Edward knows he must leave. Can he stand being alone, in the necessary absence of David during the month-long vacation? Edward will stay just for David, but he would hate to think that David couldn't invite him to his parents' house in San Jose. He would hate to think that Marlene could be the only legitimate and presentable lover in David's homophobic perception of his parents' conservatism.

"I think I'm going to break up with Marlene."

"Why?" Edward's heart begins to beat.

"I don't see our relationship going anywhere."

"Not because of me."

"No."

"I don't want to be constructed as the seductive gay man."

"Don't worry. It's nothing to do with you." Pause. "I'm actually kind of upset."

Edward wonders how upset David can really be? Is his declaration merely a heterosexual pretense? Does he actually love Marlene? Edward has a hard time imagining that David can honestly love a woman despite his claim of bisexuality, though he hates to deny the very epistemological possibility of bisexuality.

"You want to stay here for the night?"

"I should go home. I have a class early tomorrow morning."

"All right."

Then come the awkward minutes. Edward watches David get dressed and shoulder his polyester knapsack with a red ribbon dangling at the zipper. Edward walks David to the door. They kiss each other goodbye.

"If you need to talk or anything, call me, okay?" says Edward.

David nods.

The door closes. Edward feels a sudden emptiness standing alone in the living room. He feels bad about the token line he spoke earlier, "If you need to talk…" Edward is troubled by the lack of sincerity when he said it. He didn't really mean it, just as he didn't feel a bit sorry, if not selfishly and silently rejoicing. Edward can't admit that he wants David to break up with the girl, to be more exclusive despite his ideal of non-monogamy.

Edward picks up the phone and calls his cousin.

"Hello?"

"Is Victor there?"

"Who is this?"

"Edward."

"Do you know what time it is?" asks his uncle, sleepy and angry.

Around Edward's wrist, the watch reads a quarter past midnight.

"I'm sorry to wake you up, I'll call tomorrow." Edward hangs up.

The telephone rings while Edward is getting into bed.

"Did you just call?" asks Victor.

"Yeah. I just pissed your dad off again." Edward tucks his body under the blanket and switches off the lamp by the side of the bed. "So how are you?"

"Okay. And you?"

"I just had sex with Dave."

"Thanks for informing me."

Silence.

"Do you want to have lunch tomorrow?"

"Where?"

"I'll come over."

The sun has risen. Edward's eyes are open, his body in bed and warmth under the blanket. The digital clock reads 8:30 A.M. He doesn't want to get out of bed and face the chilliness. His nose is already runny. Books, manuscript pages, photocopied articles are plastered all over the floor. He has sworn to clean up his apartment some time. Today? Tomorrow? What will he do today? What books does he have to pack into his backpack? These random questions swim around in his mind. As he tries to answer them all, to sort out every banal detail…

Edward enters the house. It's empty and new. The furniture is scanty, reminding him of the interior of his mother's apartment in Hong Kong when she first moved in. He enters the living room where there is a swimming pool in the middle. The water is blue and serene, effusing a benign scent of chlorine. Edward remembers the swimming lessons that he took as a young boy. With little hesitation, he jumps into the pool. The water is suddenly inhabited with floating fungi, drowning cockroaches and passive jellyfish…

Edward's eyes open again. It's nine thirty.

"Shit."

Edward springs out of bed and gets dressed quickly.

Freshman year was the first year that Edward didn't live with his uncle. He bounced around his dormitory with a clownish smile and a loud voice. During the first week or so, when he walked by the recruitment tables of various student organizations under the brilliant Californian sun, he passed by MBLGA's (Multicultural Bisexual Lesbian and Gay Association) table and spotted the radical queers.

Edward admitted to his newfound friends that he was interested in gay and lesbian stuff. They all found Edward somewhat of a queer creature.

"I think that gay and lesbian people are fascinating," declared Edward at lunch with his friends, "but I can never imagine having anal sex because it must be kind of painful."

"Thanks for spoiling my appetite," said an Asian girl.

"I don't think there's anything really disgusting about sex, you know what I mean."

"You're just sexually frustrated," said a white guy.

They accepted Edward's queerness as normality. Edward was weird but good-natured, fun and shocking to be with. Edward played the clown's role in order to camouflage the truth that what he spoke so liberally and irresponsibly about in fact meant a lot to him inside.

"I'll sleep with my mother if I genuinely find her attractive. I don't think it's anything really taboo," declared Edward once. "Incest is a social myth."

"You're weird."

Prostitution, homosexuality, body secretions, murder and rape became Edward's trope of conversation topics. Once, his friend, a Malaysian girl, told Edward to stop trying to act weird. She said she knew that all Edward wanted was attention, but he just ended up alienating himself. A few of her girl friends had already refused to sit with Edward at the same dining table.

Once, Edward went to a screening of a local film about gay prostitution in San Francisco. He met an aspiring filmmaker in his late twenties. He was tall, kind of handsome but not exactly the type that stirred Edward's fancy. Edward once spoke with him on the phone. The man mentioned that he just came back from a gay bar.

"Are you doing some research on homosexuality?" asked Edward naively.

"No, not really—"

"You must be gay!" exclaimed Edward. "Wow!"

"Yeah," said the man, somewhat suspiciously.

"That's great. I didn't know you were gay before."

"I thought it's pretty obvious," said the man.

With a violent enthusiasm, Edward interrogated the gay man for an hour until he spelled out every sexual experience that he ever had. The man even confessed that he had a relationship with a minor, a fifteen-year-old boy, some years ago. Edward found all this so fascinating and kept asking questions until the man said, "I think I should go to bed."

Edward tried calling the man again, but the man never returned his call.

One day, Edward walked into the room and— Surprise! About ten of his floormates were there with a chocolate cake on top of which stood eighteen burning candles.

"Happy birthday to you…" they chanted.

The noise, the gossips and the sleepless nights when his roommate was typing his paper were all a hodgepodge of Edward's freshman life. He was never lonely. There were beautiful guys too. Edward would masturbate with their stolen images in the darkness under his blanket or sometimes in the shower. Sexuality was never a problem. Edward was self-sufficient. He went to see movies alone and did everything on his own. On Fridays, he would get out of class at four and went for the five o'clock show, seven o'clock show and then the nine o'clock show until his eyes were fried. He was proud, almost pompous sometimes, with so much life and hope that no one could beat him down.

There was one Filipino guy named Jesus on his floor. Knowing that Edward was a film freak, he asked Edward out to see a movie. The two boys hung out the whole day. Edward thought Jesus was kind of cute (and even cuter if all the acne had vanished from his face). They browsed through comic stores, record stores, used clothing stores and so on. When they returned to Edward's room, they were so tired that they just sprawled on the floor listening to a CD that Jesus just bought. They were flipping through comic books. Somehow Jesus started talking about his girlfriend. Edward said without a thought, "I've never had sex with a girl. Or with a guy."

"I'm not into that."

"What?" asked Edward innocently, or perhaps pretending to be innocent. "Oh. I mean… I've just never had sex with anyone."

Edward saw the suspicion in Jesus's eyes. Suddenly Edward seemed to have woken up from a dream. His hand shook as he turned the page of the comic book. There was a violent tension in the room until the door flung open and one of his roommates entered. The three boys started chatting. Not long, Jesus said he had to go back to his room to study. He took the CD out from Edward's Discman and replaced it in the case. After a brief "see you later," Jesus never went near Edward again.

"This is Ellen."

"Hi," says Victor to the intimidating and beautiful Asian girl beside Edward. Victor holds out his hand. Ellen shakes it matter-of-factly.

"So what do you feel like?" asks Edward.

"Whatever you guys want," says Victor.

"Chinese?"

The restaurant is decorated with tacky Chinese Americana including an Asian women calendar and a picture of some Oriental graphics. The Taiwanese waiter jots down their orders: Kung Pao chicken over rice, Szechwan shrimps over rice, and cold noodles. The three sit laconically each with a small cup of generic Chinese tea. Victor remains silent throughout lunch.

"What are you doing later?" Edward asks Victor.

"I don't know," says Victor.

Ellen looks at Edward's watch and says she has to catch a class. So they pay for the bill, and crack their fortune cookies. They glance over their own slips of fortune and crumple them, not caring to know of each other's fortune.

At the entrance of the restaurant, the three stand somewhat hesitantly. Ellen tells Edward to call her later, says "nice meeting you" to Victor, and walks off with a flick of her hand tossing the long dark hair to her back.

"Do you have any more classes?" asks Victor.

"No. What do you want to do?"

"I don't know."

"Do you want to hang out at my place?" asks Edward, irritated by how Victor manipulates him to play the older cousin role. If Victor wants to hang out with him, why doesn't he simply say it *straight out*?

"Sure," says Victor.

As they are walking to Edward's apartment, Victor says matter-of-factly, "Ellen is really cute."

"Yeah," says Edward, trying to camouflage his irritation. Victor's remark reminds him of other similar comments that David would make just for the sake of reinforcing his bisexuality.

Victor was expecting to have lunch with Edward alone, but Edward brought his fag hag along. During the entire lunch, Victor had to mask his discomfort. He thinks he has implied it clearly to Edward last night that he wanted to see him alone: "man to man." Did Edward do it on purpose? Could Edward be so insensitive?

Edward was docile and obedient as a child. When Victor needed Edward for any reason, Edward was always eager to help.

After all, Victor knows, more or less, that Edward loves him. He will take advantage of that.

Edward moved into the apartment (where he is living now) after his freshman year. Sick of dorm life, Edward was ready to be "independent." He was lucky enough to meet an effeminate Taiwanese senior named Robert in a drama class. Robert was the epitome of a closeted Asian male. His father owned an apartment complex a few blocks away from campus. Robert was so friendly that Edward felt his queer affection for him. As soon as he heard that Edward wanted to move out of his dorm, he kept offering his father's newly vacant apartment.

"It's really a good opportunity, you know," said Robert on the phone. "If you're not interested, many other people will take the offer immediately."

Having been turned down after applying for a few other apartments, Edward bitterly gave up his search and went with Robert's offer. With his checkbook, he went to see Robert's apartment. It turned out to be spacious, affordable and located in a nicer part of Berkeley. Robert brought Edward to see his father who spoke nothing but Mandarin tagged with occasional English words. Robert became the translator between them. The old man seemed conservative. Robert had already forewarned Edward not to act "too weird" in front of his father, since Edward had a reputation of not censoring his thoughts in class.

Edward finally had to face the quietude of living by himself. Although Robert lived only one apartment above, Edward had little desire to call on him. When Edward and Robert saw each other on the street, they would smile and say "hi." Eventually he saw less and less of Robert.

Edward's life dived into a well of solitude. He had a few friends and some acquaintances, but these friendships couldn't satisfy Edward's intense emotional need. Edward began to feel lonely, to occasionally regret leaving dorm life so early. Superficial as his dormitory acquaintances might be, they kept Edward busy.

Sometimes, Edward woke up in the morning and felt happier than the night before. He walked to buy the newspaper, clipped out newspaper articles that fascinated and inspired him, drank a café latté, ate a croissant and left for class. He hardly spoke to the familiar faces in the café, nor had he the courage to chat up those whom he was attracted to.

Once, he chased after this Chinese girl he met in his first-year English class. They would go swimming and watch movies every week or so. Edward tried to convince himself that she was a worthy object to pursue.

They exchanged Christmas gifts on the night before she flew to Hong Kong for vacation. Edward was sitting in the girl's Honda Accord parked beside his apartment. Their eyes met. She undid the seat belt. So did Edward.

Silence.

She was pretty cute, Edward thought. She was not utterly beautiful but she was presentable and attractive enough for Edward to go out with.

"So," she said with a quaint smile.

"I got you a present," said Edward and took out the polka dot scarf, boxed and wrapped at Macy's, from his knapsack.

The girl also took out a small box wrapped in reflective silver paper. They exchanged presents. Edward shook the box and tried to hear what was inside.

"You should open it before Christmas."

"Chocolates?"

"I'm not going to tell you."

"But I'll get fat," said Edward, unintentionally raising his voice an octave.

"Maybe that'll tell you what I think you need to do."

"What?"

"Gain some weight. You're skinny."

The rain started to fall in droplets against the windshield. The girl switched off the car engine.

Their eyes met again.

She let out a sigh.

Edward's heart began to pound.

What was he to do? To kiss her? No, no, Edward thought. He pretended to be resisting. Wouldn't she like him more if he resisted *that* banal temptation? Sporadically a car would pass. Its lights illuminated their faces for a brief second in the company of a dull but comforting drone.

"So what are you going to do in Hong Kong?" asked Edward.

"Shopping, studying... not that much. What are you doing for Christmas?"

"Probably have dinner with my cousin and his parents. Studying. Writing. I don't know. I'm going to be bored."

"Are you trying to make me feel bad for you?" asked the girl with a mocking smile. "Poor Edward."

"No."

"You'll be fine," said the girl. "You can come to Hong Kong if you like. Why don't you ask your mom to pay for the trip?"

"I don't want to go back to Hong Kong. I never liked it there anyway. Plus, I don't want to see my mother."

"Go see your grandmother then."

"Maybe... but I don't know. I just don't feel like going back this Christmas."

"All right, then don't complain if you're lonely."

Another car passed by. Eleven o'clock had arrived. The rain was falling lighter. The temperature in the car was dropping. The presents were still in their perspiring hands. Sweat damped the wrapping paper. Edward was holding onto the box a little too long, a little too nervously.

"I guess I'll see you after Christmas," she said with a sense of exhaustion, still kind and gentle.

"Yeah." Pause. "Thanks for the present." Pause. "Have fun in Hong Kong."

She smiled. Her hand touched the key at the ignition and turned it. Edward walked out of her car with the box of chocolates clasped tightly in his hand. He closed the door, waved to her, and watched her car glide off. With his head down, he trudged along the wet and glistening sidewalk.

That night, Edward curled up again on his bed, jacked off and went to sleep.

That Christmas was miserable. More and more, Edward realized he was *un*heterosexual. Trapped in the lonely apartment and an eventless life, Edward started a novel on male prostitution. He thought that perhaps writing would be therapeutic. The more he wrote, the more lonely he got, the more shallow and romantic he realized his art was. There was some despair.

In the name of field research, he went to Polk Street one night and sat in a café. He saw the hustlers standing on the street in the cold. One guy was wearing jean shorts. With a novel and a notebook, Edward stayed in the café for an hour or so, eyeing the prostitutes and the passing men. He went home that night and went to sleep. He thought he had learned enough just by watching. He could go on and write his novel.

Of course, his novel wasn't really the reason that Edward was back on Polk Street. The very next night, he was wearing a T-shirt, a warm leather jacket (that his mother bought him) and torn jeans. He stood at a corner before a dark shop window. Before going there, he had carefully prepared his character:

—Elliot Lim.

—Eighteen years old.

—Dropped out of high school.

—His stepfather (white) had sexually abused him.

—His real father left his mother after they arrived in America.

The first fifteen minutes standing out on the street was unbearable. Whether it was self-consciousness or paranoia, all he could feel were those disdainful glances of passersby falling upon him.

As he got colder and his skin turned dryer, Edward was no longer self-conscious. First of all, he knew he was not a prostitute. He was "a writer." Secondly, he did not believe in morality. He was a young prostitute desperately in need of money. He would go with whomever offered him the most money.

Edward felt more and more at ease with the night, with the street. He tried to meet the eyes of every potential client. Some looked back. It flattered Edward that he could in fact be an object of desire.

A cop walked by. He asked Edward what he was doing out there. Edward said he was waiting for a friend. The cop told Edward somewhat reprovingly that he could not stand there. Edward shrugged and walked up a block. The cop left in a different direction. Edward stood waiting again.

A few feet from Edward stood another hustler around his age. He was Caucasian, tall, slim, handsome but exhausted. They exchanged looks. Edward cast his eyes elsewhere. The other hustler stepped near Edward, trying not to be threatening.

"Do you have a cigarette?" asked the hustler.

"I'm sorry, I don't smoke," said Edward.

"It's kind of slow tonight."

"Really? It's my first night."

"I can tell you're a novice. Haven't seen you around before."

An older man passed by and gave one of them a look, though they didn't exactly know which one of them got the look because they were standing beside each other.

"What's your name?"

"Elliot. And yours?"

"Dan."

Not long, Edward became engrossed in a conversation with his new acquaintance. Dan was gay, and he prostituted himself every now and then for money. He just got laid off from a poorly paid waiter job, felt lazy and decided to hustle for some cash.

"How about you? Are you gay?"

"I haven't decided. But I need money."

Edward told Dan his fabricated story about his made-up parents and life. The more Edward talked, the more pleasurable he felt in lying, in creating a seamless narrative, in feeling the power of making the other person sympathize with his fictional reality.

A thin middle-aged Chinese man walked up and talked to Dan. Dan introduced Edward to the man. The man asked if Edward was Chinese, and Edward said yes. It turned out that the man, named Jonathan, was also from Hong Kong. Jonathan started talking to Edward in Cantonese. Asking Edward why he was on the street. Telling him how he *shouldn't* be on the street. Edward lied on, laughing quietly inside at the hypocrisy and moralism of the lewd Chinese man who probably wanted nothing but sex.

Dan said he was tired of standing around. Jonathan offered both Edward and Dan a lift home. The two younger men followed the older man to his brand new Toyota Camry. Dan gave Edward his phone number and said that in case Edward needed a place to stay or anything else: *Give me a call.*

"I've been through what you've been through. So..." said Dan.

Edward nodded, somewhat touched. Jonathan asked Dan where he was staying. Dan said he was staying with a friend in the Mission. As Jonathan stopped the car to drop Dan off, Dan gave Jonathan a slight pat on the shoulder before getting out. Edward moved to the front seat and strapped on the seat belt. His heart beat faster.

"So how old are you?" asked the Chinese man nonchalantly in Cantonese.

"Eighteen," said Edward.

"You know I really hate to see you out there. You're young, and you're Chinese. What would your parents say if they found out?"

"I don't see my parents anymore."

"Why're you out here?"

"I need money."

"How much do you charge?"

"How much can you afford?"

Jonathan laughed.

"How about two hundred."

"What do I have to do?"

"The usual."

"No anal sex."

"I don't do that either."

Words. Sentences. Full stops.

Edward's fingers press the keys softly. Every now and then he takes a sip of water and gently places the glass on the table. Without warning comes a shrill telephone ring. Edward scrambles for the phone in a frantic sprint.

"Hello?" whispers Edward and drags the phone into the kitchen.

"Why're you whispering?" asks David.

"Victor is asleep."

"You slept with him?"

"No!"

"I was just calling if you want to have dinner later."

"Sure." Edward glances at his watch. "Call me at six."

As Edward hangs up and returns to the living room, he looks at Victor who is lying on the futon with an innocent beauty. Edward remembers the years that they grew up together, and the mornings when they woke up together on opposite beds. There was a sense of comfort, a gentle affection.

"I'm sorry I woke you," says Edward.

"What time is it?" asks the groggy voice.

"Four."

Victor yawns. His head drops against the mattress.

"Did you have a good sleep?"

"Yeah. I did." Victor yawns. "What are you doing later?"

"I'm supposed to see Dave for dinner around six."

"I guess I better get going." Victor sits up.

"What would your parents say if they knew you were here with me instead of going to school?" asks Edward and sits beside his cousin.

"Look, I've studied and done enough for them. I deserve the right to slack off." Victor heaves a noisy breath. "You think I'm going through a phase, don't you?"

"I don't judge you."

"You're always judgmental, Edward. I know what you think about me." Pause. "Didn't I tell you that I'm not what you think I really am?"

"I know," says Edward. "How do you want me to help you?"

"Help me? I'm already your patient? I'm not sick. What makes you better than me because you're not confused? You've gone through the same shit."

Edward feels a stab at his heart. Yes, Victor is right. He has gone through the same shit. The confusion. Didn't he chase after a girl... not just one but a few. Didn't he first think he was bisexual and then come out as gay?

"You're not the only one who suffered," says Victor.

"But I had no one then."

"That's why you could come out just like that. You didn't have to care for anyone else. But I do. I live with my parents, okay? I'm not like you who can say 'Fuck you' to your mother."

"That's not the point." Blood begins to boil under his cheeks. Perhaps Edward had it easy, but not that easier. He wants to believe that he is different. He wants to believe that his suffering and pain is much greater and isolated from the petty bourgeois.

"I thought you'd understand," says Victor, trying to be less confrontational.

"Remember? That's exactly what I said to you when I told you I was gay?"

"I knew you were different, Edward. All along."

"You're so damn presumptuous."

"Not more presumptuous than you are. *You* said you knew I was different."

"Of course I did."

"You don't think that's superiority on your part?"

"You ignored me after I came out to you. You know how that made me feel? I had no one. Alone. In this apartment. Of course I wasn't traumatized by the fact that I was gay. It's just that I had no friends. Being gay made me feel more lonely. And you shut me out because you were threatened."

"I was threatened."

"You're mocking me."

"Don't shut me out. You're the only one I can turn to."

"Is that my only use?" asks Edward. "Because I'm your gay cousin and you're confused about your sexuality and therefore you… whatever. Just tell me, is that the only reason?"

"No. You're my brother."

"Victor, it's nice to feel free, even when it's lonely sometimes. Liberation entails some alienation. The point is after you're liberated yourself, after you've come out of the closet and stopped subscribing to secrets, it's really painful to carry someone else's secret around."

Victor is silent. He feels rejected.

"I don't want you to keep secrets," says Victor. "Tell my parents for all I care."

"That's not the point. The point is… it's just oppressive by itself to have to carry another person's closet."

"I'm sorry I told you."

"I'm not blaming you."

"Then what are you doing? Lecturing me about all this shit. All you're saying is that I'm closeted and I'm oppressing you. I'm sorry."

Victor rises and grabs his jacket lying on the floor.

"Don't do this to me, Victor." Edward feels weak. He can't deal with all this. He is too tired. With guilt, he approaches his cousin.

"Don't touch me!"

"Fine."

The door slams.

On the following night, Edward was back on Polk Street. He stood alone, wanting to see Dan, the hustler he had met the night before. Now he was completely at ease with lying. He felt more comfortable in his role. It seemed that this imaginary and transient life was better than his more permanently mundane one. He wanted to romanticize without the safety valve. Precisely because he could get really hurt, he stopped feeling the guilt of inauthenticity when he identified himself with the oppressed, the underclass.

A stocky white man drove by in a Cadillac and beckoned to Edward. Edward leaned on the open car window. They spoke for a brief minute. Edward hopped into the car. It was warm inside. It was one of the few times that he truly appreciated air conditioning.

"How much do you want?"

"Two hundred."

Silence.

"You give head?"

"With a condom. No anal sex."

The car stopped in the parking lot of a motel. The man told Edward to stay in the car and got out himself. Edward waited. He looked at his reflection in the mirror with a smile. A few minutes later, Edward got out and followed the man into the motel room. The man closed the door, smiled awkwardly and left the motel key on the bed. They looked at each other.

"Take a shower," instructed the man softly.

Obediently Edward went into the bathroom. Just as he was about to strip, Edward opened the bathroom door and asked if the man wanted him to get dressed or not after the shower.

"I want to undress you."

The water was cold. Naked, Edward stood outside the shower booth and waited, but the water never got warm. When he got out of the brief cold shower, his skin was all goose-pimpled. He wrapped a towel around his body, dried himself quickly and got dressed.

"Nice... nice..."

The television was on because the man was paranoid that people in the adjacent rooms would overhear them. Edward found it amusing and kept his eyes on the television screen as the stinking man ground his body against Edward's. Edward found it ironic that it was really the man who needed the shower, not him.

Unlike with the Chinese man last night, Edward could not keep his erection because the man was too physically unappealing. The man asked Edward to kiss his dick. Edward did so and put a condom over the man's scaly erect penis which was really no longer than two inches.

He did that for a while.

After half an hour of rubbing all over Edward, the man finally claimed to have come. Edward couldn't really tell. The man went into the bathroom and washed his genitals as Edward lay exhausted and disgusted on the bed. He felt good that it was over.

The man fished out two hundred dollars from his wallet. Plus an extra twenty dollar bill. Two hundred and twenty total. He told Edward that he could keep the room till the morning and was eager to set a date for next week.

"Next Wednesday."

"Sure."

"Be careful. Try to stay out of trouble," said the man before leaving the room. "I like you a lot."

It was ironic that the man just told the young hustler whom he had sex with to stay out of trouble. What kind of trouble did he mean?

It was just eleven o'clock. Edward felt too exhausted to go back on the streets. The motel room was spacious, though tackily decorated. He felt free and liberated, and wanted. He thought of calling Dan. Perhaps he could invite Dan over. Finally Edward had legitimate homosexual sex with "a man." Two men, actually. The first one was the Chinese man who was unattractive but attractive enough to make Edward come.

When Edward picked up the phone, he realized that he had left Dan's number in his apartment. Slightly disappointed, he lay back on the bed and squirmed under the cover. Strangely, he was glad to be alone for once. He turned off the lights. The sheets and blankets felt foreign. Still, it was a pleasant change.

When Edward opened his eyes again, it was morning. He turned on the television, just to let the noise fill the void in his head, and realized that it was Christmas Eve. He was to have dinner with his aunt, uncle and cousin. He took a shower and left the motel.

Edward had four hundred and twenty dollars cash in his wallet. It was all the money he had earned from prostitution so far. He didn't feel like going home. It wouldn't be an appropriate finale to his adventure.

Breakfast at Jack-in-the-Box. Downtown San Francisco. In the morning chill, Edward filled his stomach with greasy fried eggs and a muffin. It was about nine fifty. Edward sauntered along desolate Market Street, where homeless people hung out on benches and sidewalk.

Edward went into Nordstrom's, where he intended to spend his money on gifts for his uncle, aunt and Victor. He bought a portable CD player for Victor. Then he bought his uncle and aunt a box of Godiva chocolates. Time passed slowly. It was only eleven o'clock. Shoppers began to fill the streets. A Santa Claus from the Salvation Army was ringing a bell outside Macy's.

Still about two hundred dollars left. Edward went into Macy's and bought himself a half-priced Junior Gautier shirt. He went into a McDonald's bathroom and changed into the new shirt. It was almost noon. He went on the BART and headed for his uncle's house.

His uncle greeted Edward at the door. He shoved the box of chocolates into the adults' hands and shut them up with cordiality.

The sun set. Candles were lit on the dining table. Christmas Eve dinner was served: slices of turkey, cranberry sauce, steamed vegetables… all so very quaint. Edward was enjoying this flip side of life. He could only enjoy such oppressive familial ceremony as a counterpart to his recent "degrading" nocturnal adventures. Each side of his experience was a grotesque parody of the other; they came into meaning and pleasure only through contrast.

Red wine was poured into Edward's wine glass. The children, one almost eighteen and the other almost twenty, were permitted to drink on special occasions. These yellow faces, thought Edward, tried hard to ape "the civilized" West.

Edward remembered his Christmases in Hong Kong. He had always felt that he was a bad imitation of the blue-eyed little boys in *A Christmas Carol*. When Edward was preached about Christianity in his Protestant school years, he could never imagine himself to *be* a perfect Christian because Jesus always looked so pale and white as a lamb in those translated scripture text books.

"Christmas pudding?" asked his aunt.

"Just a little, thanks," said Edward.

Edward ate the Christmas pudding. He never used to like it, but he was now able to tolerate its taste and enjoy that act of eating by the very fact that Christmas pudding belonged to the ceremonious category of desserts. Similarly, Edward used to hate cinnamon when he first came to America. Unfortunately, so many desserts were flavored with that disagreeable spice, and Edward grudgingly learned to enjoy its flavor, to assimilate that foreignness into his taste buds.

It was one of the few nights in the year that Edward slept over. Almost midnight, the two boys were sleeping in one room. Sleeping with his cousin invoked both a sense of nostalgia and alienation. On one hand, Edward enjoyed the coziness of sleeping in the same room with the younger boy. On the other hand, he had to stop wanting his cousin who had estranged him.

"It's nice to see you, Edward," said the boy in the dark. "You should stay over more often."

Edward was silent, somewhat irritated by the banal benevolence that his cousin could so easily pronounce.

"Are you feeling less depressed?" asked Victor.

"Just the same," said Edward. "I'm bisexual, Victor."

"You can't be so sure."

"Because I've slept with men, and I enjoyed it."

"When?"

"Last night and the night before. I prostituted myself on Polk Street. The night before, I slept with this older Chinese guy. He was the first gay man I slept with. Kind of intense. The pure sexual pleasure, I mean. Then I slept with another man last night, but he was really gross."

Silence. Edward froze momentarily. He felt sweat on his body under the blanket.

"You're kidding me, right? You didn't prostitute yourself."

"I earned two hundred dollars from my first trick, and then another two hundred twenty from the second trick. I told you I wanted to stop believing in conventional morality, and prostitution is the only way to do this without harming other people."

"You're crazy. Why did you do it?"

"I'm writing a novel on prostitution, remember?"

"You don't have to murder someone to write a murder mystery, do you?"

"That's not the issue. The issue is I don't think prostitution is anything bad or sinful or dirty. It's so banal to believe in sins and evils. I don't believe any of it. And in order for me to prove my disbelief, I decided to try prostitution."

"You could have gotten killed."

"I'm still alive, Victor, can't you see? I practiced safe sex, no contact with bodily fluid… I used a condom for oral sex and that's about as risky as I got. I didn't get killed, murdered or raped." Edward's voice faltered. "I'm fine."

"You shouldn't have done it. You're so stupid, Edward. I just could not believe that you did something so stupid. Geez, man. I mean—"

"I've decided I'm bisexual."

"I don't care if you're bisexual. Or even if you're gay. I just think it's a very stupid and dangerous thing to do. You don't need the money, and you're just doing it for the hell of it. I just don't know what to say." A desperate sigh. "I mean I…"

"Do you think having sex with a man is as dangerous as prostitution?"

"What?"

"To you, what's the difference between homosexuality and prostitution? Tell me. You don't know the difference. They're both bad and evil to you."

"Would you keep your voice down?"

"Don't you think you enjoy what we did as much as I did?"

"You promised not to bring it up."

"Why not? Why do you condemn me to this silence? I can't even talk to you about what we did?"

"I'm straight, Edward. I'm sorry, but I'm straight. I don't know what else to tell you. I like girls. But you can do whatever you want, be whoever you are. I can't stop you from doing anything."

Edward pressed his face against the pillow and let the garment absorb his tears. He would die before he let Victor know how hurt he felt. Now, Edward was clear where he stood. His confession was a predictable disaster. He did it because he wanted to confirm his alienation and his moral superiority. He loved to see Victor's shocked reaction, to see his prediction play out exactly as he had imagined, as if it granted him more power. Control could be another form of masochism.

Christmas morning. Sunlight spilled from the kitchen window. Edward sat at the table with a cup of hot Chinese tea. When he was a child growing up in this house, he always got one present—a token one from his uncle and aunt to make him feel like part of the family. On the other hand, Victor was showered with presents—one from his mother, one from his father, one from the grandparents, his mother's side, others from his father's friends, colleagues...

Edward tried not to be jealous. He also received two large sums of money each from his grandmother and mother which enabled him to buy almost whatever he desired for Christmas. Indeed, Edward didn't need to desire that much because his cousin had everything, which he could share at will. Victor was always generous with his toys and other material things.

"Do you want to open presents?" asked his cousin in his pajamas at the doorway.

"Let me finish my tea."

Victor approached and sat beside Edward at the kitchen table. His older cousin's face seemed youthful and pretty, yet so full of bitterness and unspeakable things. That was exactly why Victor was fascinated with his cousin. Sometimes he even envied his cousin's self-destructiveness. When he called his cousin crazy, he always said it with a subtle admiration. Victor realized that he could not be crazy. He would never be allowed to be crazy.

"Look, man, I care a lot about you. You're always my cousin."

"Thanks," said Edward coldly and finished his tea.

Victor opened the present in front of his cousin. The portable CD player was an eerie surprise. He felt guilty for he only got his cousin a paperback novel. Yes, Victor had been contemplating buying a Discman, but he could never imagine that it would come from his cousin. Victor said he couldn't accept the gift because it cost too much, to which Edward lied that he got the CD player at a real bargain. In spite of his suspicion, Victor accepted the gift. He knew that the more questions he asked the more unpleasant secrets he might be bound to uncover.

Edward smiled when Victor said "Thank you." He felt a sense of silent victory over morality and hypocrisy by his subversion.

Edward stands waiting at the post office window for almost five minutes. He has little patience. The woman returns to the window with a parcel. Chewing gum, she leisurely peels off an envelope from the parcel and tells Edward to pay twenty-two dollars.

"If the content of the parcel is of no commercial value, why do I still have to pay tax on it?" asks Edward.

"I don't know." The woman shrugs. "You can call up the customs office and talk to them. I'm just here to collect the money."

"But that's ridiculous. It's marked "no value" on the slip. I didn't pay tax last time I got a parcel from Hong Kong."

"You just have to pay it, I suppose."

Grudgingly Edward fishes out his checkbook and writes a check for the amount. Having returned to his apartment, he opens the package and finds a long-sleeve black sweater that his grandmother has knit for him. How inhuman, he thinks, that the American customs office has to ruthlessly impose tax on a gift that is too valuable and personal to be priced, to be tainted by capitalism.

At seven o'clock California time, he calls up his grandmother in Hong Kong to tell her that he just received her gift. David will be here any time now. Perhaps Edward should have called his grandmother earlier, but somehow he enjoys the hectic feeling of waiting for David while talking to somebody else on the phone. After all, a long distance call couldn't possibly last that long.

"I'm glad you like the sweater," says his grandmother. "I've already started on another one for you."

He feels valued by his grandmother, but simultaneously embarrassed by her pampering.

"Are you coming back to Hong Kong this Christmas?"

"I think so. Ma's paying for the ticket."

"If she doesn't, I will," says his grandmother at once. "I hope to see you. After all, I'm old and I don't think I have that long to live. But if you have something else to do, don't let me hold you back."

"I'll come." Yes, someone could hold Edward back here, only that someone does not bother to hold him back. It's better for him to go. To be alone for those few weeks of Christmas vacation.

"I have a lot of things to tell you if you come back," says his grandmother. "Since you like writing, I have some memoirs to tell you. Only if you're interested, of course."

They say bye to each other and hang up. It's five minutes past seven. David still hasn't shown up. Edward replaces the receiver languorously. He sits before the computer and tries to write, but he can't because he's too obsessed by anticipation.

The lateness is soon unbearable. It's already half past seven. David said he would come over at seven. Edward flops against the bed.

He finally decides to call David. He picks up the phone and dials the number.

Goddamn answering machine.

The doorbell did not wake Edward. It's eight thirty. Edward braces himself up from the bed. His head is weighed with a temporary dizziness. All is dark. He hears the distant siren of an ambulance. He rises from the bed and picks up the phone.

The answering machine again.

"Fuck," mutters Edward under his breath. A violent but helpless anger fills him for a moment. Then he feels rejected. Why does this have to happen?

The telephone rings.

"Hello?" Edward's voice is shaking. "What's up, Victor?"

"I just called to see how you are?"

"I feel awful," says Edward. "Dave is one and a half hour late."

Then the doorbell rings. It must be David. Edward tells Victor that he'll call him back and hangs up. After all, David shows up. "Hi," he says. "I'm sorry. Something came up."

"What came up?" is the immediate question Edward wants to ask. But he checks his tongue. He lets David in without verbally accepting his apology. Edward sits on the bed. David paces around the room.

"Do you want to go eat?" asks David.

"Sure," says Edward, swallowing the discontent gorging at his throat.

Eating in an Indian restaurant, Edward is still unsettled on the matter. David has not yet explained why he was late. He takes a sip of Chai which scalds his tongue. Something is wrong, but David remains silent. If he could be content with silence, he would rather let it pass. Throughout the dinner, Edward's mood is teetering on the edge. Edward appears to be absent-minded. He feels alienated by his own silence. He answers all the mundane questions that David asks, trying to control his temper.

"You seem out of it tonight," says David.

"I'm just tired," says Edward. Why did he just lie?

The dessert arrives. David has ordered a syrupy Indian pastry. He forks out a bite and offers it to Edward, feeding it into Edward's mouth. A moment of sweetness.

Out on the street, David holds Edward's hand. The sudden gentleness renders Edward more hesitant to confront David. They walk along the street, hand in hand. California breezes brush their faces. Edward's fingers feel the soft skin of David's palm.

"Do you want to come over?" asks David.

"All right," says Edward.

"Okay."

They walk on for a block or more. Still holding hands. Not talking too much. Edward looks at the illuminated signs and store windows. Trying to stop appearing uncomfortable. But he is uncomfortable. How long will this temporary effort of comfort last?

"I'm really pissed that you were one and a half hour late without giving me a call," says Edward calmly. "It's very irresponsible."

A significant silence before David opens his mouth. "We stayed a little too long in the park," he says. "We" means *them*: David and his "straight friends" who were tripping on acid earlier in the afternoon.

"You could have called."

"I'm sorry."

"It makes me feel very insignificant. I feel hurt, you know." Edward swallows and says, "Don't do that to me again."

"Okay."

"I don't want to act like a bitch or something. But one and a half hour is really quite late, you know…"

Silence.

"Do you think I'm paranoid?" asks Edward.

"Paranoid about what?"

"Do you think what I demand is reasonable?"

"No," says David softly. "But a lot of people can't even comply to very basic and reasonable demands."

"Why do you think so?"

"I don't know."

Their hands part as they arrive at David's apartment building. David fishes out his key from his pocket and opens the glass door. In the apartment lounge his housemate Mike and his straight friends. Mike is a chummy white male who is "fascinated" with Japanese culture. Mike is ethnically suspicious, Edward thinks, but he is liberal enough to accept David's bisexuality. Mike's friends say "hi" to the two queer boys.

Undressing.

Naked bodies touching.

Saliva.

Edward cannot decide if their sex is becoming routine or more comforting. Edward sometimes wonders how they could be more creative in bed; but he fears that this desire for creativity precisely confirms that their sex can so easily turn into a routine, and that their relationship is highly dependent on sex.

"Do I irritate you sometimes?" asks David.

"Why do you think you irritate me?"

"Because I can tell. When you try so hard not to keep calm, not to show irritation."

"It's probably when you promise to do something and then do it half-heartedly. That's what irritates me most. If you can't do something, or don't want to do it, just tell me. I'm only asking for honesty."

Silence.

"Are you feeling better about you and Marlene?"

"Yeah, I guess," says David.

The words slowly sink into silence. Each silence between them stretches on longer than the one before. Their eyes close. Their consciousness fades from the physical world of intimacy. Edward remembers that the saddest moments of his childhood were those when he woke up after dreaming about his friends. In the darkness, alone in his bed filled with lifeless stuffed animals, he realized that his friends had only been a figment of his own imagination. Whatever he and his friends talked about in the dream was only a monologue trapped within himself. It made him so much more conscious of his alienation, of his need for real companionship.

Even now, in the same bed with an intimate friend, Edward still has to retreat to his unconsciousness where he is alone.

How much of David is part of Edward's imaginary construction?

A week had passed after Victor opened the Christmas present that Edward gave him. His uncle called, and invited Edward over to his house for dinner. Somewhat reluctantly, Edward went. Edward sensed a strangeness from his uncle when he entered the house. The man was more cordial than usual, while the woman seemed uncomfortable and out-of-it. His cousin was not there. The two adults sat the prodigal child in the living room where the inquest began.

"I don't really know what to say, Chung Tuck," said his uncle, sitting on the couch with one foot on his knee.

His aunt placed a cup of tea beside Edward and sat with her husband facing the boy.

"What do you mean?" asked Edward, puzzled.

"Victor told us what you did."

"What?"

"Well, what you did on those two nights before Christmas Eve."

"Why did he tell you?"

"He was so worried about you, Chung Tuck. Don't get mad at him. He thought about it for a long time before he decided to tell us," said his aunt.

Edward let out a sigh and waited for the adults to open their mouths again.

"Just promise us not to do it again. All right? We care about you a lot," said his aunt.

"It's my body. I can do whatever I please."

"Do whatever you please?" His uncle exploded. "Who do you think we are? We have no obligation to give a shit about you if you want to become a degenerate and get AIDS."

His aunt added immediately, "All we're saying is that you should be more responsible, because if you do get sick it is us who will end up having to take care of you."

"I practice safe sex."

"Safe sex?" his uncle snorted. "What sex is safe if you go have sex with some strangers from the street? You can be so stupid, sometimes. All I'm saying is that if you get AIDS, don't expect *us* to take care of you. Remember, we've warned you. It's your fault if you grab shit and smear it upon yourself."

"You don't have to take care of me," said Edward. "I'll kill myself before I come to you."

"Chung Tuck! Don't say that!"

For a moment Edward thought the blood in his heart had suddenly dried up. The adults were sitting before him. A thin film of tears covered his eyes. The once most private subjectivity that he had was no longer his.

"Are you gay?" asked his uncle, suddenly shifting from Cantonese to English.

Edward brushed the back of his hand briskly over his eyes. His vision was blurred. He quickly wiped his eyes again, trying to be as nonchalant as possible.

"It's okay, tell us," said his aunt. "We won't love you any less."

No matter how amoral or strong Edward had believed himself to be, before these adults (Chinese, patriarchal and blood-related) Edward lost his complete independent rationality and became a confused child. He was overwhelmed by memories of past helplessness as a child in that house.

He wanted to get up and leave. But he just sat there and confessed his sexual ambiguity.

Not gay. Perhaps bisexual.

He didn't know yet.

As soon as the confession took place, he felt the violent desire to be approved and to gain these adults' sympathy.

His uncle told him to be careful, and said that he hoped he *would not* be a homosexual. His aunt echoed a similar version of what her husband had spoken though her words were weathered with more kindness. The adults took the boy to dinner. His cousin was not there. When Edward asked about Victor, his aunt told him that Victor had gone out to dinner with some friends.

They went to a Hong Kong style café ran by a Chinese American family not far from the house. The Asian waitress came to take their order with a smile. She had mistaken Edward as Victor. The couple corrected her at once.

"This is our nephew."

His uncle ordered half a roast chicken. His aunt ordered linguini with veal. Edward ordered spaghetti with tomato sauce. They ate like a family. By and by, Edward regained strength as his stomach was filling up. He was thinking clearer. More detached. Less vulnerable.

"How's your studying?"

"Not bad," said Edward and sipped his water.

"I'm sure he's keeping up his A's at Berkeley," said his aunt. "We're proud of you, Chung Tuck."

After dinner, the three walked into the cool night toward the Mercedes. His uncle drove Edward to the BART station. He felt sad when he was waiting for the BART to arrive. It was about nine o'clock on a Saturday night. He thought of his lonely apartment, and then of Victor whom he loved and who betrayed him. He told Victor about his prostitution only because he wanted to share some part of his subjectivity with him—a secret.

How could he talk to Victor again?

Edward finally admitted that he was in love with Victor at that moment.

The train arrived.

Sitting in the empty car, Edward caught his reflection on the window. When he got out of the BART station, he was out in the night again. Cold air filled his lungs. He walked toward Polk Street. He didn't know why he was doing it.

There were other hustlers on the street. All older and very exhausted. Edward wondered if Dan was around. He went inside a porn store where he browsed through gay porn magazines. On the cover of a jack-off magazine, a title made Edward uncomfortable: *Hustlers of Hong Kong*. His eyes stayed on the words for a second or two. He looked away and decided that he wasn't interested in anything about Hong Kong, about his nativity.

He remembered, as a child growing up in the colony, he had always felt white people to be more beautiful and European culture superior. He was studying English now. He heard of some friends who were into Asian American and African American literature. Minority and racism stuff. He wasn't at all interested. He believed in the Artist and the Individual. He didn't want to marginalize himself. He wanted to be a great writer. His literary subjectivity was dominated by dead white males.

He remembered someone had once told him that he was "white-washed." Although he had forgotten the face, the voice haunted his mind every so often like a phantom echo.

Edward was standing on the street. Waiting. He was getting cold. He was beginning to wonder why he was standing here. Did he need the money? Did he want to have sex with another disgusting old white man?

Pacing to and fro, Edward struggled for the strength to depart. A car pulled up beside him. Inside sat another fat older man. The man pointed a finger at Edward.

As the car drove off, Edward started to walk down the street. With his head down, Edward kept walking faster. Quickening up his steps, he was no longer in the hustler zone. He was walking beside the City Hall, where its lofty columns and stone sculptures were lit up. A few minutes later, he was at the BART station. A homeless person was crouching at the entrance.

"Spare some change?" asked the homeless man.

Edward delved out some coins from his pocket and dropped them in the man's hand. He was on the train again. In the warmth and protection of interiority, he knew exactly why he turned back.

"So what do you think?" asks Edward.

"I think it's good," says Ellen and puts down the essay.

"Do you think it's pretentious?"

"No, I think it's quite honest and to the point," said Ellen. "Although I'm afraid that the admission committee may have some conservative people on it. You'll have to take that into consideration."

"But if you were in my position, would you identify yourself as gay."

"I don't think so, because being gay is still kind of too marginal," says Ellen. "I don't think it's a label as exploitable as Asian American or African American... you know what I mean?"

"Yeah." Edward ponders.

"It's also Yale, you know. You're probably going to be judged by conservative heterosexual white men."

"On the other hand, I've heard that Yale is supposed to be very progressive and queer."

"Maybe," says Ellen. "You should send it if you believe in it. But it's just kind of risky. Hit or miss depending on the committee. But what do you care? You're going to film school, right?"

"Yeah. I'll just send it."

"Don't worry," says Ellen. "I'm sure you'll get into one of the schools. Your application is so strong."

"I hope so."

"You can't afford to doubt yourself now." Ellen rises from her bed and picks up her pack of cigarettes. "Do you want to talk outside?"

Edward follows Ellen out to the small balcony. Ellen sits on the steps of the fire escape and lights a cigarette. She flicks away the few strings of long hair irritating her face. She exhales a cone of smoke which quickly dissipates in the air. The whiteness of the cigarette is contrasted against the redness of her painted lips. Edward can't help associating the cigarette with the phallus. Of course Ellen isn't smoking to compensate for her lack of a penis, but smoking does lend her a more anti-feminine and rebellious image.

"I wish there was someone I could have a crush on," says Ellen.

Ellen takes a puff of her cigarette. The sky is turning twilight blue.

"I always have crushes on guys," says Edward, "but they're usually straight or for whatever reason unattainable. I honestly don't think I have that high standards. I just want someone relatively cute and nice. But I'm sure that *you* can pretty much get whoever you want."

"You have to understand, Edward, it's not necessarily that you're less attractive or anything. It's just that there are a lot of guys who are closeted and confused. It's easier to be heterosexual, but not that much easier because finding someone you can really click with is difficult."

"I know." Sigh. "I don't know what to do with Dave."

"Just stop analyzing so much. No wonder you're always so exhausted. Dave is a relatively nice guy, and he's cute. But let's face it, Edward, this is transient. You have to move on eventually. When you leave for grad school, he'll still be here. Just have fun and enjoy the moment."

"Sometimes I think that's what I want, but the instability and insecurity really drive me crazy. I wonder if I really need that much freedom. Or even non-monogamy. I may be perfectly satisfied with Dave alone."

"You'll find someone you really love. And when you find him, all the past relationships and sufferings will be insignificant."

4

Analysis

"Hello, Edward," said the overweight woman sitting on a chair before the couch, where Edward sat with his hands on his lap and his backpack beside his foot.

"I'm Diana."

The wall was painted pastel orange. There was a table in the room. On top of the table were a lamp and a vase of roses. On a wall hung a framed crayon drawing of a woman. Probably drawn by a child. Edward wondered if Diana was married, and if it was her child who drew the picture.

Sitting neatly on Diana's lap was a file. *His file* containing pages waiting to be filled.

"What would you like to talk about?" asked Diana.

"I feel unsure about my sexuality."

"Do you think you may be gay?"

"Yeah, but that's not what I'm too concerned about."

Pause.

The lengthened pause became silence.

Eyes met.

Still silent.

"What concerns you?" asked Diana at last.

"I feel uncomfortable about silence. I always have to fill up the silence with words. I can't explain it, but when nobody talks, it bothers me."

Diana nodded.

Silence.

"You know what I mean?"

Diana nodded.

Silence.

Edward couldn't help laughing. Then he felt embarrassed. Diana's face remained unmoved. What was she thinking? Edward couldn't bear it and spoke again, "I came to see a therapist because… because I'm also bothered by some sexual experience I've had some weeks ago."

"Would you care to tell me your experience?"

"I prostituted myself to two older men." A sigh. More air needed to fill those demanding lungs. More words to be spoken. "I told my cousin about it, and he told my uncle and aunt. They asked me if I was gay." Pause. "Since then I've been feeling…"

Diana did not speak. She looked at Edward during his speechlessness, awaiting his next articulation. It irritated Edward, because Edward felt the compulsory and helpless desire to fill the semantic void.

Shortly, he heard his voice again.

"I know it sounds ridiculous and unreasonable, but I've been feeling strange. It's like I think I have AIDS."

The fifty minutes passed. Edward walked out of Diana's office and toward the receptionist's desk where the appointment book was lying wide open. The receptionist gave Edward an appointment for next week.

Same day. Same time. He walked out of Cowell Hospital. Down the red brick stairs. A breeze of cool wind passed him. He felt a little dizzy and everything was a little blurred.

As a child in Hong Kong, he had thought that only nut cases went to see therapists. When Edward came over here, psychiatrists were such popular figures in movies and TV. There was a time in high school when Edward thought that having a therapist was a hip thing. A few of his high school friends boasted about their emotional problems, harrowing depressions and expensive psychiatrists.

The dark apartment. The dirty laundry. The chaotic books. The unpublished manuscripts. You could easily make a list out of each element of disarray which reflected Edward's hopelessness. He was becoming more and more paranoid. His desk was filled with information sheets and pamphlets on AIDS. These pages spoke to him about his potential symptoms—white spots on the tongue, purplish to brownish lesions on the skin, night sweat, swollen lymph glands, weight loss.

When Edward was studying, he would start feeling under his jaw for his lymph glands. Every time he did so he could not decide if they were swollen or not. At a certain time of the night he would start getting a headache. He felt tired and unmotivated. He had a hard time trying to get to sleep. He feared taking a shower because he didn't want to see his decaying body. He couldn't look at himself in the mirror when he was in the bathroom. He would take a brief shower, step out and dry his body as quickly as he could.

Edward returned to see Diana again. He started to trust her, but not completely. Prostitution was a foil to the deeper problems that Edward did not want to touch: his roots. These roots were all entwined together in the most random and chaotic fashion, clawing onto his heart.

"I don't have anyone to love," said Edward, softly, close to tears. At the corner of his eyes lay a box of Kleenex. Diana had expected her patient to break down. And for that very reason, Edward refused to. He held back.

"I don't quite understand what you mean by that," said Diana.

Silence. Edward felt more comfortable with silence now. He no longer felt the imperative to fill it with words. He took the moment of silence to contemplate. To reflect on himself without the unconscious fear of inexistence.

"I hate my mother." Pause. "I guess I don't hate her but I just can't love her."

"Are they separated?"

"My father died in a car accident. My mother remarried another man."

"Are you angry at her because of the new marriage?"

Silence.

"No. I'm angry at her because she never gave a shit about me. I was raised by a nursemaid. I was closer to her than to my mother. Frankly, I like my stepfather more than my mother. I went back to attend their wedding about five years ago. I… I really had a hard time accepting her. And I had some very perverted thoughts."

Silence.

Edward continued, "I wanted to seduce my stepfather. Even though I didn't really find him attractive."

"It was the power that attracted you, wasn't it?"

"Yeah," said Edward. "I wanted to feel I had more power than she had. I wanted to feel as physically attractive as she was. You know, as a child, everyone I met, including my classmates, told me that my mother was beautiful."

"You're jealous of your mother."

"Do you think it's easier to love people in America because love is so popularized? You see it on TV… I mean it's harder to express love in

Chinese culture because we just don't say 'I love you' to each other." Pause. "Do you love your mother?"

"Edward, we're here to talk about your relationship with your mother. My relationship with my mother is irrelevant."

"I'm sorry," said Edward coldly. "I should know."

"What do you mean?"

"You're a therapist. You don't *really* care."

"Why do you say that?"

"Because you're paid to listen to me."

When the session ended, Edward made another appointment for next week. He had been through three sessions, and he had yet seven sessions left. Each Berkeley student had ten free therapy sessions.

Days were better than nights. Edward was haunted by paranoia in the lightlessness of his apartment. A tiny spot on his body (for example, a fading scar of a mosquito bite) could make Edward sweat in fear. His body appeared more and more grotesque.

The semester was passing slowly. Edward returned to Diana week after week. Sometimes the sessions seemed to make him feel better afterward (but only for a very temporary period); and sometimes he felt they did nothing for him. After nights of sleeplessness, headaches and irrational fear, Edward decided to see a doctor. The doctor examined him and said that Edward might be hyperventilating.

Of course, Edward didn't mention to the doctor that he thought he had AIDS. He didn't say so because if he did he would give in to his imaginary state of disease. He knew it was paranoia, but he just couldn't break out of the illusion. In the daytime, he would feel fine and healthy. But as darkness set in…

One day he saw a flyer on campus about a sexual orientation rap group for men. He went one night, after weeks of deliberation. He was there five minutes early, and sat in a circle of chairs. The coordinator introduced himself to the new closeted boy with a book on his lap. When the chairs were filled by mostly students, some older and some younger, the discussion began.

"I'm Edward. I'm here because I feel kind of traumatized after I prostituted myself," said Edward.

Everyone nodded. Someone else spoke. That night's topic was something like "coming out to your family." Edward hardly participated in the discussion since no one else seemed to address "his trauma." After an hour, the coordinator called for a wrap. Edward was extremely disappointed. Everyone said his name again.

Edward rose from the chair. They all seemed to know one another. They laughed and chatted about things and people that Edward had no bearing on. None of them even bothered to cast a glance at him.

The night was cold. A street artist was playing a trombone at a corner. Café windows and neon signs were the only colorful illuminations. With his hands in his pockets, Edward hurried home and went to sleep.

San Francisco's shop windows are once again filled with Christmas decorations. Salvation Army Santa Clauses stand at street corners. You can hear the bells in their white gloved hands ringing amidst the traffic and noise of Market Street. Today is the last day before Edward's departure. David still has an exam tomorrow afternoon, but he has dinner with Edward anyway.

Inside an Ethiopian restaurant on Telegraph Avenue, they sit facing each other and use their hands to scoop up the food with a thin pancake-like cooked dough.

"So when are you coming back?"

"January the nineteenth."

"Hm."

"Are you driving to Texas with Ricardo?"

David nods. "I'll be back before you."

Silence.

"You know something?"

Edward looks into David's eyes

"You know I used to find you intimidating to talk to?" asks David.

"Why?" asks Edward.

"When I first met you, I couldn't understand why you would want to be my friend. You're this artist, writer, an English major. And I'm a science person. I figured that everything I said would sound stupid to you."

"Do you still feel the same way?"

"A little, maybe."

"I've always respected you. I listen to everything you say. Do I talk too much when I'm with you?"

When they walk out of the restaurant, David holds Edward's hand. Coupling closely beside each other, they walk up Telegraph Avenue.

The car's windshield fogs up. David turns up the fan to defog the glass. Once again they are crossing the Bay Bridge. No music but silence, comforting but somber. A glowing green highway sign zooms past above them. The car glides off onto an exit ramp.

The engine is still running. Now is their parting moment outside Edward's uncle's suburban house. It is more convenient to stay there because Edward is taking an early morning flight from San Francisco. David undoes his safety belt. Edward follows. Their eyes meet. David's eyes seem so expressionless and indiscernible. Could it actually be a relief that Edward is leaving?

This very moment reminds Edward of a similar but different moment some years ago… when the girl Edward dated drove him home on the night before she was to leave for Hong Kong. The difference is that there was no desire or passion then.

Edward hugs David. They kiss each other's dry lips soon moistened by saliva. Their tongues touch each other in a very cursory contact.

"Have a good trip, Edward." David kisses Edward again… deeper this time.

Just as Edward is about to get out, he says, "Dave."

They look at each other for a silent moment. Edward feels vulnerable.

"Have a fun trip," says Edward and gets out.

It's cold outside. The trunk pops up. Edward takes his suitcase and backpack out. After waving David goodbye, Edward toils up the stairs to the front door of his uncle's house.

Past midnight. Edward is wide awake on the sofa bed in the basement. His uncle has put him in the basement so that he can leave soundlessly through the garage early next morning. Or is it? Has he ever slept in his cousin's room since two years ago after he came out? He shifts in the bed and closes his eyes. Not sleepy. His head is weighed with anxiety about the open possibilities that he's leaving behind.

"Edward?" asks a voice in the dark.

Edward starts up and sees his cousin standing a few feet from him. Barefoot and wearing pajamas, Victor approaches and whispers, "May I?"

Silence implies approval. Victor slips under the blanket beside Edward. One of his cold feet touches Edward's thigh. Edward shrinks slightly. Victor folds an arm around Edward's bare back and draws them closer.

"If they find out, they'll kill me."

"They'll kill me too," whispers Victor. "But they'll never find out."

Their bodies are pressing against each other's. Victor's smell has changed. As Edward recalls, a long time ago, it was the smell of soap. Now Victor gives off a stronger odor, something more characteristically male.

"But what?"

Their breaths cross each other's. Victor closes his teeth on Edward's earlobe. An intruding tongue in his ear sends a pulse of pleasurable shivers through Edward.

"Do you like it?"

"It feels neat."

"Do you want me to stop?"

"I don't know," says Edward.

Their erections are protruding out of the elastic bands around their briefs.

"Your skin is still so smooth," says Victor.

"You too."

Victor's hand fondles Edward's back in a series of pressing motions. Victor tunnels another arm under Edward's armpit. They shift slightly so that they are comfortably fitting into each other's body contours.

"I want to kiss you."

An inch of air separates their lips. Edward's lips draw closer and touch Victor's passive ones.

"You don't have to."

Victor kisses Edward, somewhat forced. Then again. Their sexual passion rises as they hump against each other. Edward unbuttons Victor's shirt so quickly that he tears one of the buttons.

"I want you to fuck me, Edward."

"Why don't you go for an HIV test?" Diana asked in her customary cool and insightful voice.

"Because I know it's my imagination, and by actually going in for the test, I would give in to my paranoia," said Edward, sitting more at ease than the last few times he had been in the room.

"I don't see why you shouldn't get tested if it will make you feel less paranoid."

"Can we talk about something else?"

"Sure." Then Diana added, "Before I forget to tell you, next week will be our last session."

"It is?"

Diana nodded. "If you want to consider continuing our sessions, you'll have to make some arrangement with the university health service."

"Do you think I need to continue?"

"What do you think? Do you feel it's been helpful to come here?"

"I don't know," said Edward.

Silence.

Edward left the office with the decision that he would not continue after the last free session expired. It was lunch time, and he felt hungry. He went to a café and ordered a latté and a muffin for lunch. He knew he wasn't eating proper lunch, but he took immense pleasure in doing that. When Edward finished his food, his stomach was temporarily barely full. He knew when he got back to his apartment his stomach would feel empty again.

He enjoyed hunger. It was an aesthetic feeling, a kind of guiltlessness.

His mother called as soon as he got home. "Hello? Chung Tuck?" Her voice sounded distant.

Edward greeted his mother in Cantonese. They spoke for a little less than five minutes...

"Just to see how you are doing," said his mother.

Edward let out an "Um," a backchannelling in Cantonese that sounded like an animal's grunt to Westerners.

Silence. Edward compared this silence to that in Diana's office. His fingers played with the telephone cord. He wondered what his mother would think if he told her that he was seeing a therapist.

"Do you have anything special to tell me?" It was one last routine question that she asked every time. Edward usually replied, "No, not really," after a few seconds of forced hesitation.

"I'm gay," said Edward matter-of-factly in English.

"What did you say?" asked his mother in Cantonese.

"I'm gay," repeated Edward in English. "I've made up my mind. I thought I was bisexual, but I am gay."

"Are you doing this to shock me?" in Cantonese.

"No." Edward replied. "But you don't have to care. It's my life. I'm only telling you because I'm tired of you asking me about girlfriends."

"You're joking."

"Whatever you think."

"You are so..." muttered his mother with a voice charged with accusation. She started screaming, "You want to drive me crazy, don't you? You want to irritate me, that's all you want to do. You are just—"

Edward hung up. His heart was beating hard. His hand was still holding tightly onto the cordless. His mother had not screamed at him since he left for America.

The piercing telephone ring startled Edward. Without choice, he picked up the phone.

"Why did you hang up on me?"

"Because you were screaming."

"Don't you ever hang up on me, you understand?"

"Stop screaming at me, or I'll hang up."

"Have you forgotten who I am? I am your mother. I gave you birth. Don't you dare to think we're equal."

Edward heard his mother's vague sobbing.

"Look what you've done to me, you bastard. You'll get struck by lightning."

Still, Edward did not speak but clawed silently onto the receiver.

"I don't care about you anymore. You can be a homosexual. Go ahead. I always knew you would do something like this," she continued with sporadic sobs interjected with swells of anger. "Are you happy at last?"

"Don't make me feel guilty, Ma."

"You are guilty," replied his mother in English. "You think you're so good that you argue with me in English?"

"Whatever you say," Edward switched back to Cantonese. "Are you finished?"

His mother hung up.

"What time is it?" asks Edward.

"Late," says Victor in the dark. "What time is your flight tomorrow?"

"Eight."

Victor inches up to steal a glance at the alarm clock by the bedside: one thirty in the morning.

"I'll get plenty of sleep on the plane," says Edward and folds an arm around Victor. Victor kisses Edward's arm.

"Did you like it?" asks Victor.

"Yeah. Did you?"

"Uh huh." Pause. "I'm going to have to go back upstairs. I'm afraid that I'll fall asleep with you here."

"Wouldn't that be wonderful? If your father comes down and sees us in bed together?"

"You have a sick imagination," says Victor.

"It's romantic. Don't you think?"

With a half laugh, Victor sits up beside the horizontal Edward. He looks at his older cousin whose youthful face displays such an ironic innocence. Edward reaches to touch Victor's shoulder. Victor holds Edward's hand with a smile in the dark.

"Have a good trip."

Victor gets up from the bed.

After his mother hung up on Edward, he left the house and went to class. He stayed in a café after the class ended. It was only four o'clock then.

An hour later, he was in Cody's Books browsing through shelves after shelves of books, from Children's corner to Travel section. At seven, he went to the Berkeley Free Clinic where anonymous AIDS tests were offered.

In the lounge, among a group of fifteen young queer men sat Edward with a *Cinefantastique* magazine. A queeny white man in his mid-thirties stepped in and asked, "AIDS test every one?"

"Yes," muttered an almost unanimous voice.

"Line up this way, girls," said the white man with flamboyance.

The air was lightened. Giggling and chatting with one another, the men formed an orderly line outside the doorway of a room where blood samples were taken. Edward smiled as he heard the other people laugh at some joke that he didn't catch. A young gay man turned to Edward with a brief glance and a smile. There was some solidarity in this smile.

Edward's turn had come. He was led into the room where there were four comfortable chairs. Edward sat before a Chicano woman with a dyky haircut and an ACT-UP T-shirt.

"So how are you today?"

"Not bad."

"Good." She smiled and knelt before Edward with a clipboard. "We're going to give you a number. When you come in to get your result next week, you'll use that number. And in order for you to be eligible to take a test, you have to consent to pre-test and post-test counseling."

"What do you mean?"

"We're going to ask you a few questions before the test. And when you come in, a counselor will give you the result. That's about it."

"All right."

The few questions were quickly spent. Edward's heart beat quicker as he caught a glimpse of the needle and empty test tube in the woman's hand. She tied a rubber tube around Edward's forearm while his elbow was resting on a side-table beside the chair.

The woman smiled and rubbed alcohol onto the skin above the vein at the crook of Edward's elbow. "It's not going to hurt."

Edward turned his head sideways, focusing his eyes on the wall. A pinch. His heart was beating. Edward remembered a scene in a science-fiction film where someone was shot in an environment of no gravity. The outflow of blood became blobs of red liquid floating in the air.

"Press your finger here."

Edward's finger pressed against the small mass of cotton over the needle wound. The tubes were filled with his blood.

When Edward walked out of the clinic, he felt light and happy. It was at that moment that his vision of the night, of everything around him, recovered its clear boundaries. He no longer had a headache. He no longer felt tired. He no longer had the fear.

When he returned home, he found no messages on the answering machine. He thought of his mother whom he pissed off earlier in the day. How could he tell her that he went through an AIDS test, and that he felt good about it?

Edward was hungry, but there was nothing substantial in the refrigerator. He finished the few remaining non-fat cookies and drank some diet coke. It was no dinner, but Edward was satisfied. He sat in front of his computer and tried to write. He began a new novel.

The telephone rang. It was his uncle who had just received a call from his "mad sister" in Hong Kong.

"Why're you so selfish, Chung Tuck?" asked his uncle, extremely agitated. "Your mother just screamed at me on the phone like a mad woman."

"It's between her and me."

"You really think it's that simple? You are really stupid if you do. You made us worry so much after you told Victor what you did. And then, you did this. It's just really irresponsible of you. Keep your dirty laundry to yourself. We're not interested about how you degrade yourself."

"I'm sorry."

With a grunt his uncle hung up.

Weeks came and went. The day of Edward's last appointment with Diana arrived. It was three hours after the original appointment when Edward remembered about it.

"Shit," he muttered to himself.

He shrugged and continued down the street. He thought perhaps he should call up Diana and tell her that he missed the session *not* because of any conscious effort; he had simply forgotten.

He forgot to call Diana too.

His HIV test result came back. The counselor flipped open Edward's file quickly and closed it.

"Although it turned out negative this time, you should continue to keep testing and practice safe sex. All right?"

With an erection uncomfortably constrained under his jeans, Edward wakes up sitting in the half-reposed seat inside the plane's dark compartment. He looks at his watch. It's twelve o'clock California time. His head is still heavy with dizziness. Victor enters his mind. He doesn't really feel guilty about what they did even though he wants to. Guilt will make it so much more incestuous and romantic.

Then he thinks of David. He shouldn't feel guilty about their relationship. Why should he? David has never been monogamous anyway. He knows that David will end up sleeping with Ricardo (David's ex a year ago) on their road trip. David can never resist anything. How much will things change when Edward returns after the vacation?

The rest of the waking moments pass sluggishly. When Edward tries to read, he can't suppress the excitement when Victor's body drifts into his mind.

It's a relief to get off the plane at last. He can smell the drab stench of his clothes while he is standing in line to go through the immigration checkpoint. He chooses the line with the sign "Hong Kong residents."

When the immigration officer asks him a question in Cantonese, Edward cannot speak for a second. He awkwardly answers him in Cantonese.

He spots his mother, with her usual make-up, gaudy fashion and all, standing beside his stepfather. They both smile. Edward waves to them as he is pushing his luggage down the ramp flanked by yellow faces. Hong Kong natives: men standing beside their wives, children clinging onto the aluminum railings, all anticipating.

His mother kisses him on the cheek. His stepfather shakes his hand.

Insulated inside the car, Edward feels a temporary relief from all the crowd. Then he is "home." The empty room awaits him: a bed, a desk and a closet. His suitcases are lying on the floor. He sits on the bed and takes a deep breath.

He calls up his grandmother. He calls up Man Wai. His heart is beating. Man Wai's mother answers the phone. She recognizes Edward's voice, and says that she will leave a message for him.

Holding onto the cordless phone, Edward wonders who else he can call. Nobody. The excitement ends. He lays the phone on the bed.

"Come out for some soup," says his mother at the doorway.

Edward follows his mother out to the dining room where his stepfather is seated at the table with a smile. His mother sits down with Edward. Out of the kitchen comes the Filipino maid with three bowls of soup.

"What soup is it?"

"Chicken," says his mother. "Are you hungry? I'll tell her to make you some instant noodles."

"I'm fine," says Edward.

"So I heard that you've applied to graduate schools," says his stepfather.

"Yeah," replies Edward, "I hope I'll get into one of them."

"I'm sure you will. Your mother says you're doing very well at Berkeley."

"And how's everything else?"

"I'm seeing this guy," says Edward nonchalantly, "He's pretty cool. We're kind of getting along."

"Do you see your uncle and aunt often?"

"I saw them before I left. I spent the night at their place." Edward says, "They seem fine."

Silence. Edward picks up the spoon and starts sipping the soup. His mother watches him. She too picks up the spoon and starts sipping.

Edward wakes up at seven thirty A.M. Jet lag. He tosses on a T-shirt and wanders into the living room. The Filipino maid is setting a place at the dining table. She smiles slightly and says "Good morning" to Edward.

The Filipino maid puts *The South China Morning Post* beside the place mat and returns to the kitchen. Edward sits on the chair beside the place mat and picks up the newspaper. He flips through it: a thin newspaper compared to *The San Francisco Chronicle*.

"Morning, Edward," says a male voice behind him.

"Morning," says Edward. He turns around and sees his stepfather.

The white man sits at the place already set for him. Edward folds the newspaper back into its original form and leaves it for his stepfather to read.

"You don't have to," says his stepfather.

"Oh, I'm finished with it."

"So what's your plan for the afternoon?"

"I may go to lunch with my grandmother and then see my friend Man Wai."

"We're really happy that you're back."

"Me too."

"You should perhaps talk to your mother a little more. She cares a lot for you."

"I'll try."

"I know how this sounds to you. But do think of me as someone you can talk to. It's difficult for us both, your mother and I, to have to figure out how you feel about things in the dark. Talk to us."

Edward nods. His stepfather is silent. The Filipino maid brings out a cup of coffee, a grapefruit, and a doughnut for Clifford. She asks if Edward wants breakfast. Edward asks for a cup of coffee.

Clifford has left for work. Edward sits in the living room with two English phone books (one residential, and the other commercial) and starts searching for gay and lesbian resources. Nothing under "Social Organizations." Nothing "gay" or "lesbian." He looks under "Night Clubs" but cannot figure out which club or discotheque sounds queer.

His mother makes her appearance at eleven o'clock and eats her breakfast: two glasses of water (to maintain her delicate skin), a glass of orange juice, a banana and a slice of toast. She talks to Edward briefly, asks him about his agenda for the day, and retreats back into her room after her breakfast.

At twelve o'clock, Edward still has no clue where gay people can be found. He throws on a shirt and a pair of slacks. Sitting in the back of the taxi, Edward watches people and cars in passing. The news comes on the radio. English names are translated into Cantonese. It takes Edward a moment before he recognizes George Bush's name.

His grandmother is standing outside Hong Kong Club wearing red high heels and dark sunglasses. She waves at Edward as soon as he steps off the taxi. Edward tunnels his arm under hers and escorts inside the club.

Not far from the table where Edward and his grandmother sit, there is another table of two Chinese ladies. The restaurant is practically empty: one English woman here and two English men there.

"There was not one Chinese member in this club when I first joined," says his grandmother. "Not one."

"So how did you get the membership then?" Edward asks and tears a corner off the slice of French baguette.

"Uncle Harry was a member, and since I married him I was also enrolled as a member." His grandmother takes a sip of water. "How's the buffet?"

"Great."

"Do you still like Western food more than Chinese food?"

"Depends on my mood."

Edward nods and puts a baby tomato in his mouth. Both of them eat meagerly. The old woman naturally has little appetite, while the young man is idiosyncratic. She takes a plate of dessert and places it before Edward who soon abandons the resistance. He takes a miniature chocolate pastry and puts it in his mouth. He looks at the buildings outside the glass walls of the restaurant. He thinks of David, and Victor, and Ellen, who all exist on the other side of the world.

"Do you want coffee?" asks his grandmother.

"Do you?" asks her grandson.

"I'll have coffee if you do."

"Sure."

The waiter brings two cups of coffee and sets them on the table with a sugar bowl and a jug of cream. In addition, Edward asks for Nutrasweet.

"Do you plan to stay in America?" asks his grandmother.

"I want to work in Los Angeles, since that's where the film industry is."

His grandmother nods. "Do you have a friend there?"

"A friend?"

"An intimate friend."

"Yeah," says Edward. His heart starts beating.

"Is (she) cute?"

Edward realizes that he can continue to "lie" because Cantonese pronouns are not gendered. It is only when his grandmother mentions the word "girl" will he have the opportunity to...

"(He) is cute."

"Don't get married so early. Of course, Grandma is not in the position to tell you what to do. I couldn't even ask my son to do anything. But make sure it's really what you want before you make any hasty decision. Play is fun. But if she gets pregnant, then it's not fun anymore. It becomes an obligation."

"Was my mother pregnant before their marriage?"

"No," she says with a reassuring smile, "but your father did rush things too quickly. He didn't even finish his university degree and he wanted to get married. If I had been your mother, I would have encouraged my boyfriend to finish his degree. Well, but I guess she must have told him that he could still make money without a degree."

A pause.

"After your grandfather died, he left me nothing. I had to work at Uncle Harry's place to support your father's schooling. But the past is the past. And I'm glad you like studying. It's important. I've never had the opportunity myself to do what you're doing now."

Silence.

"Grandma," says Edward, "I'm going out with a guy. I'm homosexual."

"Are you playing a trick on me?"

"No."

His grandmother nods. "It's all right. I don't mind. I'm open-minded."

That is all.

He must have been four or even younger. There were three rooms in the apartment, and his room was not large. Edward dreamt of the fourth room. A new room that he did not know of before. A doorway opened up on the wall behind his bed that he could crawl through and enter this new space.

Then there were the memories of his parents who would come into the room and kiss him goodnight at a very late hour. They must have just returned from some function or party. Edward always pretended to be asleep. His eyes remained shut, but he could feel the contact of his parents' lips on his cheek, which was a very foreign feeling.

Edward was set to wander in shopping malls while his mother and father were trying out clothes for hours. After those few hours, Edward would return and tell his father what he had wanted to buy, some toy or whatever. The adults would go into the toy store, shell out and pay.

Edward grew out of banal materialism quickly after he came to America, where he turned to writing, to reading, to consuming arts and other cultural abstractions.

At last Edward is able to locate the phone number of a newly forming gay and lesbian hotline in Hong Kong. He bugged *The South China Morning Post*, reporters after reporters, explications after identifications, over and over again: "I am gay, I want more information on gay organizations." All these people were skeptical in giving out phone numbers because of the stigmatizing and oppressive atmosphere of the colony.

To Edward's disappointment, it is a man with a British accent who returns his call. There will be an organizational meeting at a gay bar in Tsim Sha Tsui. A gay bar? Although Edward is tired of the club and bar scene in America, he cannot suppress the excitement of making contact with the gay community in his *very own native* land.

Edward tells his mother that he won't be home for dinner and that he will be going to a gay bar for an organizational meeting. Knowing that Edward will do whatever he pleases, his mother says, "Be careful," which prompts Edward to ask, "Be careful? Of what?"

"I don't know," says his mother. "Those places."

Edward sits beside the chauffeur, a Filipino man, in the car. How much he loathes the class-conscious and bourgeois arrogance of his mother who always sits in the back seat.

Paulina grew up in a lower-middle-class family and married an upper-middle-class man. She worships the high and tramples the low. Edward used to hate his mother for calling his nursemaid "uneducated" and "lacking common sense."

"So how do you like Hong Kong so far?" Edward attempts to strike up a conversation with the Filipino man.

"It's okay," replies the Filipino man.

"Have you been back to the Philippines lately?"

"I'm going back this summer."

"To visit your family?"

"My wife and two children."

"Cool."

A married man...

Edward finds out that the man has a degree in architecture from the University of Manila and he used to play jazz in a band. Nevertheless, he came to Hong Kong to drive a Chinese woman.

"My best friend," says Edward, trying to suppress a nostalgic sentiment for Peter, "is also Filipino. He also plays in the jazz group at my school."

The car pulls to a stop beside the MTR station. Edward says "Thanks" and gets off. He feels slightly irritated by himself, by his conscious attempt to befriend the chauffeur, whom he objectifies as the subaltern. Isn't he doing the same thing that his mother does?

He walks under the densely packed neon signs above his heads. The shop windows are filled with cameras, VCRs, camcorders and illuminated signs of brand names such as Sony, Toshiba, JVC and Panasonic.

At last he finds the right street number and enters a commercial building. He sees the sign at the door: Yellow Magic, 6th Floor. He pushes the button for the elevator—waiting... somewhat impatiently, nervously, excited.

The elevator door opens.

Edward looks at his watch and realizes that he is fifteen minutes early. Timidly he steps into the bar decorated with cheesy Western motifs. Above the bar against the wall are the words YELLOW MAGIC painted in a semi-artistic script. There is a piano on an elevated platform that resembles a shrunken dance floor. TV monitors are hung at the corners of the wall, showing a Karaoke video of the Grasshoppers, a popular Hong Kong boys band.

A waiter in a yellow uniform approaches Edward. It seems that he can't sit here without buying a drink.

"Perrier, please," says Edward, the first word in English, the second in Cantonese.

Edward settles down at table and looks around. A few Chinese men sit at scattered tables; none of them stirs Edward's fancy. At the bar work two cute boyish waiters chatting with a white man about his Motorola portable phone, a status symbol in Hong Kong.

The glass in Edward's hand is almost empty. Edward always finishes his drink too soon. He glances at his watch again: almost time. Two men step in the bar—one younger, the other older. They glance around and whisper something to each other. They take seats at a table. Edward finds the younger one cute. He has dark skin and he wears glasses: somewhat dorky and school-boyish. Edward wonders if they are here for the meeting.

A stocky white man in his late forties enters with a briefcase. He stands near the entrance and looks around. He seems to be the man in charge. The two men, whom Edward has been scamming on, approach the white man. Another man follows.

Edward does the same.

"Hi, are you Perry?" asks Edward, "I'm Edward. I spoke with you on the phone."

"Pleased to meet you," says the white man in a diplomatic way and shakes Edward hands.

Another young white man dressed in a suit enters and greets them. The group proceeds to the balcony, where they set up a circle of stools. Two more Chinese men show up, both wearing executive clothes.

Perry takes out a thin pile of photocopied agendas from his briefcase. The two Chinese men, whom Edward has been scamming on, whisper to each other. Everyone waits for the agenda to be passed around. With an English accent, Perry tells everyone to introduce themselves around the circle. Edward catches the name of the young man he is curious about: Simon.

As Mark (the other white man) opens his mouth, Edward recognizes an American accent. Almost immediately, Edward feels more solidarity toward the American than the English.

The English man talks on, about setting up committees, appointing treasurers, coordinating volunteers and training phone counselors. He has made several references to London where he himself was part of a gay and lesbian phone line organization.

"We will be the first organization in Hong Kong to achieve the official status of a non-profit gay organization..."

Of course everyone listens attentively. It reminds Edward of an authoritarian classroom under the colonial claw. He realizes that the Chinese must listen very attentively (except for Edward and Mark who are both educated in the U.S.) because they have to struggle so hard with an intimidating language.

Edward remembers that feeling.

"I think," says Edward politely, "it would be a good idea to get more participation from the lesbian community."

"Of course," says Perry, "but unfortunately, they have been relatively passive. Though I think we have one lesbian who is interested to get involved."

Edward sinks back to silence. He retains his skepticism. Can he trust a white man to lead the first legitimate gay organization in the culturally colonized Hong Kong? Then Edward wonders if he truly has the right to criticize. After all, he no longer lives here.

The meeting is painfully bureaucratic. Edward has volunteered to draft the organization's constitution with Mark. Simon and Kenneth will be the treasurers. Although Edward is bored, he dreads the end of the meeting. He lingers around after the meeting. The Chinese men start chatting in Cantonese. Edward stands listening and waiting. Then Simon and Kenneth start leaving, so do the rest. Edward follows.

"So what's your name?" asks Kenneth with a Chinglish accent.

"Edward. I speak Cantonese," says Edward in Cantonese.

"I told you he knew how to speak Cantonese," says Simon.

Chatting, the three of them leave Yellow Magic. Edward tells Simon and Kenneth that he has just arrived from Berkeley, and that he was born in Hong Kong. Kenneth tells Edward to visit Club Yin Yang in Central, though he claims that he rarely goes there. Just before Edward parts with them, he asks for their phone numbers. Matter-of-factly, Kenneth and Simon write down their phone numbers on a sheet of paper and hand it to Edward. Edward also gives them his phone number.

Edward enters the MTR station with a gush of satisfaction. Edward looks at his watch: only eleven o'clock. He decides to check out Club Yin Yang. Out of the MTR station in Central, Edward calls the operator for Club Yin Yang's number, then he calls the club for the address.

Toiling up the slope of Ice House Street, Edward arrives at the small but slickly designed entrance of Club Yin Yang. He sees a well dressed Chinese man at the counter atop which sits a sign: $50 TONIGHT.

"This is a gay club, right?" asks Edward.

The Chinese man nods.

There is an empty dance floor with the dimensions of a twin-size bed, a bar behind which waiters are serving drinks, mirrored columns and stools. The Karaoke lounge is

insulated with glass walls. Edward stands at a corner and surveys the environment. A fortyish white man is standing not far from him. Some middle-aged Chinese men are sitting around with beer bottles in their hands.

There are younger men, though Edward does not find them especially attractive. A few people start dancing in a circle. Edward sits down on a stool and fixes his eyes on the lightless ground. He feels uncomfortable, stiff, socially dysfunctional and very self-conscious.

More people come. Some young women: probably fag hags. One or two cute guys. Everyone dances in pairs or closed circles. It seems likes everyone knows each other, which makes Edward an absolute outsider. But he can pass, can't he? He looks like one of them. Yellow skin. Young. He can even speak the same language.

"What's your name?" asks the white man beside Edward.

"Edward."

The white man nods with a smile. He is tall, almost bald and with a slightly visible belly, wearing a white shirt and blue jeans.

"I'm Michael, nice to meet you."

English. Edward can tell from his accent. He shakes hands with Michael.

"Do you go to school?" asks Michael.

Edward nods.

"You speak very excellent English," says Michael amidst the loud music.

"I study English."

"At University of Hong Kong or Chinese University?"

"I go to school in the States."

The conversation simmers. Edward appears to be visibly uninterested. The white man eventually excuses himself. Edward sits there, looking up and looking down. Smoke flows out of lips and squirms in the air. Edward wants to dance, but no one seems to be dancing alone on the dance floor.

Almost an hour has passed. Edward sits turning into a mannequin at a dark corner. At half past midnight, Edward gets his butt off the stool and walks out of the club. He hails down a taxi on the street and gets in. The taxi driver presses the button on the meter and steps on the gas. Edward sits peering out of the window, watching the passing scenery of concrete constructions.

The streets are empty in Central. The traffic lights change from red to green. Edward can still smell the pungent smokiness clinging onto his clothes. He thinks of David, and of Victor, and of Hong Kong, where people only dance in closed circles.

David is going to have sex with Ricardo. Edward just knows so. Yet what right does he have to be jealous? Edward just slept with Victor.

At the least, he hopes David will tell him. Honesty is all Edward demands.

Edward's mother was born of a lower-middle-class family in Hong Kong. She grew up with her two brothers, one older and the other younger. While her older brother went to Columbia University for his undergraduate years, she became an air stewardess through a training program at BOAC.

Edward's grandmother (his father's mother) was born in a poor family in a small village. Her uncle attempted to sell the girl when she was six years old. At twelve, she decided to help support her family by learning to be a singer in tea houses. She ended up hopping from brothel to brothel for the next few years.

Not until Edward's mother became an air stewardess did she adopt an English name: Paulina. She met Edward's father one year after she started flying. Edward's father was a man soaked in salt water (having studied in England) and now a medical student at Hong Kong University. They were introduced by a mutual friend who recommended Edward's father to be her English tutor.

Many men drifted by his grandmother's life. She was pregnant once by a business man at Shanghai. The baby died three months after it was born. She wept. By then she had bought herself out of the brothel life and was working as a companion at dance halls. She learned how to dance and entertain men. She met her first love: a university student. They burnt passionately for a few months until the man's family forced him to get married with some decent girl. The student's mother tried to bribe "the young whore" with a check: *Don't marry my son, please.* Edward's grandmother tore the check into pieces and never saw her first love again.

Paulina was in her second year at BOAC when Edward's father proposed. She initially refused. Edward's father threatened suicide. He threatened to starve himself to death. Paulina agreed to marry him at last and to quit her job. Edward's father did not want his wife to work, to mingle with the worldly.

Edward's grandmother eventually came to Hong Kong, where men from Shanghai were still running after her. Many wealthy Hong Kong men also had their eyes on her. She married Edward's grandfather (a man who owned a Rolls Royce, two sailboats, and a personal jet) on the promise that he would support her mother and father, who eventually died or lost contact with her during the Cultural Revolution. Edward's grandmother gave birth to two girls and one boy. When Edward's father was in his late teens, Edward's grandfather (whom Edward had never seen) passed away and left his wife widowed.

When Edward's father told his mother about getting married with Paulina, Edward's grandmother aired her disapproval because he had not finished his university education. He should have waited for just two more years. Edward's father married Paulina anyway. He was in love.

After the death of Edward's grandfather, the widowed woman was left with almost no money and property except for the Rolls Royce. Edward's grandfather had too many debts and his estate recommended a declaration of bankruptcy. In the constant fear of facelessness, Edward's grandmother struggled to maintain the family income by knitting sweaters and working as a maid in order to send her children to school. She ended up marrying a white man for whom she had worked as a maid. Her children violently disapproved of the marriage. Little did they know, she was marrying for them.

The marriage between Edward's father and his mother took place at a church. Lavish Chinese banquets followed. All paid out of Edward's grandmother's pocket. She bought the newlyweds an apartment and a car. She also paid for their honeymoon. Although Edward's father had dropped out of school, Paulina assured her husband that he could still make money without a degree.

A year after her son's marriage, her first grandson, Edward, crawled out of Paulina's womb.

"This is really depressing here," sighs Edward on the phone. "I mean everyone in Hong Kong is so cliquish."

"Edward, you're only going to be there for a couple more weeks," says Ellen. "Why should you care about those lame people? You live here now."

"But I still believe— I don't know. I don't really belong anywhere. Not in the place I was born, and not in America. I feel so delegitimized. You know what I mean?"

"I think the strategy is to realize that no one really belongs to anywhere. Belonging requires you to blindly follow a patriotic illusion. For you and I, Edward, we'll always be marginalized to a degree no matter where we go."

Silence. "I think I better go. It's going to get really expensive."

"All right. Don't let it drag you down. Have fun." She adds, "Oh, I saw Dave on the street the other day."

"Was he with anyone?"

"No," says Ellen and takes a puff of her cigarette. "I think this is good for you. By the time you get back, you'll have more distance. At the same time, this will also give him an opportunity to realize that you're valuable."

Edward hangs up in the dim living room of the apartment beside a small lamp. His mother and stepfather are probably asleep.

The sun rises and sets. Edward passes his days by going to lunch appointments at hotels with his native high school friends (including Man Wai) who are now studying in England or America. He sees his grandmother whenever he gets a chance. He feels closer to her.

Edward has also started preparing the constitution with Mark who turns out to be talkative and amiable. Mark has a lover. The two of them have adopted two children from the Philippines.

When Edward gets home after one long day of wandering in the streets, he finds a message from Simon. He is suddenly filled with excitement. He takes a deep breath to calm his pounding heart and picks up the phone. A woman answers the phone, and then Simon comes on the line.

"I just thought I'd call you up and see what you're up to. I don't have school tomorrow."

"Do you want to see a movie?"

"All right."

Edward is five minutes early at the Tsim Sha Tsui harbor. He stands above the slow movements of waterlogged garbage pushing against the dock. He is both nervous and excited. Simon shows up on time, wearing jeans and a windbreaker. Edward approaches with a smile.

They buy their tickets for the two o'clock showing of *A Nightmare on Elm Street Part V*. Of course, when the film ends, Edward is disappointed. Unlike in Berkeley where he would immediately bitch and vomit critical jargons as soon as the end credits roll, Edward remains discreet and quiet. It isn't only because he is shy before Simon. He simply lacks the critical vocabulary in Cantonese.

Now, they are suddenly faced with the necessity to decide where they'll go to next. Edward invites Simon to his mother's place. Simon accepts, and they take the ferry to Central.

"How long are you going to stay here?" asks Simon beside Edward, who is peering toward the approaching shore of Hong Kong Island.

"For another two and a half weeks," says Edward. "How old are you?"

From the childish awe on Edward's face, Simon guesses that Edward is very young, much younger than him.

"Twenty-two," says Simon.

"I'm twenty-one," says Edward.

"Are you seeing anyone in America?"

"I guess I can say that. We're not... *committed*," Edward has to use an English word, "our relationship isn't *closed*. You know what I mean?"

Simon nods.

"Are you seeing Kenneth?"

"Yeah," says Simon matter-of-factly. "We've been together for almost a year."

"That's good," says Edward with a vague smile.

Getting off the ferry, they take a taxi to Edward's parents' apartment. There are silences, and Edward, as always, feels the urge to fill them up though he remains very controlled and calm.

Before the window in the living room, Edward and Simon look out to the almost empty beach of Repulse Bay. They are both thinking. The green sea water laps against the sand. The crests of the waves are occasionally whitened in their rushing against the shore.

"So your parents live in Hong Kong?" asks Simon.

"My father has passed away. My mother and my stepfather live here. He is American." Edward asks, "I'm sorry. I forgot to offer you anything. Do you want something to drink?"

"No, I'm fine."

By and by, they drift into Edward's room. They sit on the edge of the bed. Edward takes off his shoes and pulls his feet up onto the mattress.

Some tension…

"Do you miss your boyfriend?" asks Simon.

"I guess a little. But I'll see him soon." Edward pauses. "Do you love Kenneth?"

"I don't know," says Simon. "He complains that he's willing to die for me and I don't love him enough. And his ex-boyfriend wants to get back together with him." Pause. "Kenneth whines a lot. Sometimes I think he's too immature, even though he's five years older than me. I just can't tell him that I love him so much that I can die for him. It's too melodramatic. I'm just not that kind of a person."

"I fooled around with my younger cousin the night before I left for Hong Kong."

"Your younger cousin?"

"He's two years younger, and I've been having such a crush on him since I was fifteen. We fooled around before, but we stopped. After I told him I was gay, he became very… *homophobic*. Then about a month ago, he told me he was bisexual. I spent the night at his place before I flew back to Hong Kong, and it happened."

"When I met you, I got the feeling that you might be a playboy type."

"Why?"

"You look like the type who fools around."

"I thought I looked innocent."

Simon smiles.

The white man returns home from work and finds the two young men in his house. He asks if they want to have dinner with him and his wife.

Edward replies, "Sure."

At dinner, Simon is slightly intimidated in the presence of Edward's parents, especially the white man who speaks nothing but English.

Even though Edward realizes that his stepfather might find him rude, he talks to Simon in Cantonese. He enjoys the power that he can code-switch from English to Cantonese and vice-versa at will. He feels a momentary mastery over both cultures. Of course, he also perversely enjoys intimidating the white man by speaking a language that he can't understand.

After dinner, Simon calls Kenneth to meet for coffee. Edward says bye to his parents and leaves with Simon after grabbing a light jacket.

"Your mother is really beautiful," says Simon while they are in the elevator.

"Everyone says that my mother and I look alike. But she's the one who always gets the compliments."

"You're jealous, aren't you?"

"Not jealous. It's just that I sometimes think I'd look better if I were a woman."

Edward and Simon step out of the taxi at Central. They meet Kenneth in a small jazz café near Lan Kwai Fong where fags, foreigners and expatriates roam. When they enter the café, he sees two suspiciously queer couple, a white man and an Asian man, sitting at a corner, and says to Simon, "Are they gay?"

Both the white man and the Asian man throw an annoyed glare at Edward. Simon hits Edward on the shoulder.

"This is not America," says Simon.

Kenneth just laughs. Edward shrugs and says unabashedly in English, "I'm gay too."

Sitting there, Simon watches Edward talk so lively and so excited. He is amused at Edward's constant attempts to suppress the spontaneous outflow of English words, and the way he carefully translates his English intellectual jargons into near-nonsense Cantonese. Edward is cute, Simon thinks, but he knows better than to get involved with a fleeting Westernized Chinese boy from America.

Simon remembers the few hours that he spent with Edward alone earlier in the day. They *could have* done something.

The three leave the café around midnight, since Kenneth has work and Simon has school tomorrow. The two native queers walk Edward to Landmark where he can find a taxi. Edward gets inside the car and waves goodbye to them. Alone now, Simon and Kenneth walk into the MTR station.

"You seem happy with Edward," says Kenneth matter-of-factly.

"Would you please stop sucking on dry vinegar?" says Simon coldly. "We're just friends."

"Edward's a nice guy. He's quite *cute* too."

The train arrives and the doors glide open. Kenneth and Simon enter and sit uncomfortably beside each other under the public eye of heterosexuality.

Dear Edward,

I hope you're not upset about the amount of time that we haven't communicated. I tried to call you twice, but nobody answered. I am very confused about the time difference. Ellen told me Korea is sixteen hours ahead, but I thought it was actually ten.

I told you before that I admire creative artists more than anyone else, so you must know that you are very inspirational to me. I have been trying to write a short story for the last two days, and it is really fun. However, I have no way of knowing whether it will be even slightly interesting to people other than myself.

Of course, I cannot write a letter as literary as yours. My trip with Ricardo was lots of fun. On the way I made as few stops as possible, and I wrote the other letter in here on the only night that I got full rest. We went to a proto-rave in Houston and hung out with his sisters and their friends.

They assigned me a guest room at Ricardo's house that adjoined his room. I never slept in it. On the first night we slept together without doing anything, as was our previous custom. Every night after that was more and more intense. On the way back we had a lot of motel sex, and during one two-day span I came five times, which I thought was a lot.

How is your vacation so far? I saw Ellen on the street and she told me briefly that you thought gay people in Hong Kong are cliquish and snobbish. I hope you're having a better time now. I had already finished the candies you sent me. They were really good.

I checked your mail and messages. Your cousin called twice, wondering when you're coming back. You received a heavy package from Crossing Press. Call me when you know the details of your flight.

Have fun. Be a happy boy.

Yours,

David Wong.

Edward refolds the letter neatly and re-inserts it into the envelope. He is disappointed at how predictable people are. Victor crosses his mind for a second. He tries to convince himself that he got equal with David by sleeping with Victor.

After his cousin left for Berkeley, Victor had made up his mind to be heterosexual and popular. He knew he had the looks. He joined the basketball team, won some mathematics competitions, went to parties and drank beer with his friends. He succeeded to be *normal*. He went out with girls. He even slept with one before graduating from high school, which had been one of his goals: to sleep with a white girl.

At home, he was obedient and chummy with his father just like the white American kids on soaps. His father made jokes. Victor laughed and joked back. His mother seemed pleased when Victor closed his door and studied in his room. He even showed interest in what his parents wanted him to study in college. He was going to be pre-med (something like molecular biology or chemistry) and then go on to medical school.

However, Victor was very conscious of his own construction, of all the expectations that his parents hammered over him. Most of his consciousness came from Edward. As a child, he heard what his father said about his cousin and knew his father had irrational prejudice against Edward simply because of Edward's mother. As much as he knew that his cousin suffered silently, he also knew that his father loved him blindly.

Like a privileged spectator, Victor saw the action behind the stage. Edward hated living there, yet day after day the boy must pretend to be happy, content and satisfied before the adults. Edward was lucky enough to have left the house for college. Victor remained there after graduating from high school.

Victor continued to play his part. Sometimes he began to confuse his true self with the part that he was playing. Perhaps there was no truth after all. No original. Everything was merely an imitation, a copy.

Victor passed as straight. He could almost pass as white, since most of his friends were white. Unlike Edward's, Victor's physicality and gestures were perfectly masculine and untainted with queerness. His language and voice were unmarked while Edward still had a slight Hong Kong accent.

Deep down, Victor knew that he couldn't be the perfect American boy. Contradictions arose again and again ever since he could remember: when he was confronted with his face in the mirror, when he was confronted with his invisibility in *GQ* magazines, TV, movies, etc. But Victor learned to live within contradictions and the illusion of normality. Stifling as it might be, Victor would rather conform than become an alien like Edward. After all, why should all-Americanness be denied from him? After all, Victor was born on American soil.

In the dim sum restaurant at the airport sit Edward's mother and stepfather with his parting son and two friends. Edward is still gay. His mother is still distressed. His stepfather still attempts to remain outside. Kenneth and Simon are still together, though their relationship is wearing thinner by the day. The dim sum waitresses (such a sexist job, isn't it?) push around carts loaded with greasy delights. Edward chopsticks a shrimp dumpling and dips it in soy sauce. His stepfather eats meagerly. The meal is more of a ritual than anything else.

When Edward once again leaves Paulina, she feels empty and sad. Her son has left her with two younger men who are so irrelevant.

"Shall I give you a ride?" his mother asks Kenneth and Simon in Cantonese.

"No, it's fine. We'll manage," says Simon.

"No, really, it's on the way."

"All right, thanks," says Kenneth.

The two gay men are sitting in the back of the car while the heterosexual couple is in the front.

"Are you two still in school?" asks the mother in the passenger seat.

"I'm at City Polytechnic, and Kenneth is working," says Simon.

The woman nods. The white man drives silently. Simon sees Paulina's face reflected in the rearview mirror. It is drawn with some anxiety and unrest. Simon, too, feels a certain sadness.

"Aunty, you shouldn't worry about Edward too much," says Simon. "He's doing quite well on his own."

"I hope so," says the woman, surprised at the younger man's sensitivity. "I'm just not a good mother. I can't talk to him, and he seems just a little too strange."

"He's very Westernized," says Simon, "but he's really a good person. Although I don't know him for that long, I can tell he cares about things, and he knows what he is doing."

"I hope so," echoes the woman.

Crossing to the other side of the world, Edward closes his eyes and convinces himself that another chapter of his life is closed. Simon is in Hong Kong. He is glad that he has made a good friend. He is tired, so he takes the sleeping pill that his grandmother gave him for the plane trip.

Edward has made up his mind to settle in America. Hong Kong has become a phantasmatic homeland, one that almost doesn't exist, like paradise, like hell, a place of past cultural transit.

His grandmother's words float into his mind. Even though his mother has given up on him, he has strong support from his grandmother both financially and emotionally. Her love and assurance make Edward feel safe.

When Edward gets off the plane, David is waiting at the gate. They hug after a very brief second of indecision. Edward says he is hungry, so they drive to Chinatown for lunch. When they get out of the car parked in an underground garage, David casually takes Edward's hand. Holding hands, they saunter along in Chinatown and enter a Chinese restaurant for noodles, sitting face to face. Edward feels more assured.

"So are you tired?" asks David.

"No, I slept the whole way on the plane."

"So you missed the meals?"

"I hate airplane food."

"It's my favorite!"

"I should have brought it in my knapsack for you."

"Yeah," says David with a childish grin.

Silence. David looks in the direction of the cashier, where a few Chinese youths are paying for some take-outs. Edward follows David's gaze.

"That guy is cute," David turns to Edward.

"Which one?"

"The one smoking."

Edward catches a slim Asian guy with glasses smoking a cigarette among his friends. He feels a slip of insecurity in his heart.

"I guess he's cute," says Edward.

David nods and chopsticks a Chinese broccoli onto Edward's plate.

"Eat."

David looks in the cashier's direction again as Edward swallows the masticated fiber down his throat and drinks a gulp of tea. When David returns his eyes at Edward, Edward says, "You're kind of obvious, aren't you?"

"I like looking," says David.

"I do too, but I try not to. Because I don't want to make the other person uncomfortable. I mean I'd look but I'd look away really quickly."

David takes Edward to the apartment afterward. It's three o'clock in the afternoon. David puts on a New Order CD and lounges on the couch. Edward feels awkward, but he sits beside David anyway. David puts his foot on Edward's lap and hums to "Bizarre Love Triangle."

"Are you happy?" asks David.

"Are you?"

"Reasonably," says David.

"I can't tell if I'm happy or not."

"I like you a lot, you know."

Edward smiles skeptically. What about Ricardo? And other guys whom David finds cute? Is Edward too paranoid, too insecure?

"I've never thought of a non-exclusive relationship before you," says David and inches closer to Edward. "You make me think about so many things."

Unable to resist intimacy, Edward lays his head beside David's. It's so much easier, so less painful, to give in. Physics quietly steals over language. David puts his arm around Edward. Diffused sunlight spills from the window, bleaching a side of David's already pale face.

"What are you thinking?" asks David.

"Nothing. What are you thinking?"

"Nothing," says David with a mocking smile.

"Stop mocking me."

Silence. They hold each other tighter and lay their chins on each other's shoulder. Edward brushes his lips against David's neck. David licks Edward under his jaw. Edward throws his head back.

"How's your cousin?"

"He's okay," says Edward, and kisses David. Edward misses the perfumed smell of David's deodorant.

At about four o'clock, Edward walks back to his own apartment alone. Sex was over. They have kissed each other goodbye. Edward unlocks his apartment door and encounters a familiar scent. Edward is glad that he tidied his place up before leaving for Hong Kong. A neat home makes the end of his trip less of a down.

Alone now, he feels the emptiness gnawing at him from within. He feels irritated by his dependency on David. He knows David is going to see Ricardo tonight. That was why Edward felt the implicated necessity for him to leave David's apartment earlier. He stands above his desk and glances over the letters atop. Nothing too important. He listens to the messages on his answering machine. Ellen called. Victor called. A few silent messages.

Edward picks up the phone and dials his cousin's number. He reaches his uncle's answering machine. Instead of hanging up, he leaves a message for Victor, "Hi, this message is for Victor. It's Edward. I just got back from Hong Kong. So… give me a call. Bye."

When he hangs up, his heart starts beating.

Edward calls Ellen next.

Answering machine again.

Edward leaves a message.

5

The Others

One night, Victor lied to his parents that he was going out to see a movie with Jennifer. He drove by the O'Farrell Theater, a heterosexual strip joint where he and his straight male friends once went before. Along Polk Street, the slow cruising car ahead of him allowed Victor to have a good look at the men standing out on the street. When Victor passed the hustlers zone, he turned onto a side street. His car slowed down on the desolate road. His heart was beating ever so quickly.

In the rearview mirror, he noticed a police car approaching from behind. He took a deep breath and stepped on the gas pedal. He didn't break any law. Why should he feel so paranoid? Victor looked in the rearview mirror again. The police car was behind his tail. He checked his speed limit.

The warning siren startled him. In the rearview mirror, Victor saw the revolving red and blue lights on top of the police car. His heart jumped. Victor took a deep breath, suppressed his nervousness, and pulled up beside the curb.

A policewoman got out of the police car with a flashlight and stepped toward his car. For the brief moment that he had, Victor fixed the Cal cap that he was wearing. He calmly rolled down the window and faced the expressionless face of the white woman.

"May I see your license?" asked the policewoman.

"Sure." Victor fished out the license from his wallet. "I wasn't speeding, was I?"

"Where are you going?" asked the policewoman after examining Victor's license.

"Home."

"Did you drink?"

"No."

"You forgot to turn on your lights."

"Oh," said Victor with a charming smile and checked his light switch. "You're right. I'm sorry."

"That's okay. Just drive carefully." The policewoman handed Victor back his license.

Victor rolled up the window and watched the policewoman walk back to her car in the rearview mirror. He turned on his headlights and drove forward slowly. The red-and-blue lights on top of the police car faded into the darkness.

As soon as he got home, Jennifer King called. Victor intercepted it just in time before his parents got to the phone. Victor opened his lips. His voice sounded out of breath. As the conversation went on, he seemed very distracted.

"Victor?"

"Yeah."

"What's wrong?"

"I'm just tired."

"Oh, I see."

Silence.

"So what about tomorrow night? I mean we could maybe…"

"Oh, I'm sorry. I'm supposed to be having dinner with my aunt from New Jersey." Victor was becoming a compulsive liar. "I'm not sure what time I'll finish. How about if I call you tomorrow night?"

"You *are* going to call, aren't you?"

"Of course."

"All right. You better get some sleep then."

"Yeah."

"Good night."

"I love you," sang Victor matter-of-factly and hung up. Sometimes, he found Jennifer such a pain to talk to. He went out with her because she was objectively attractive. Many guys had their eyes on her, but she wasn't an easy lay. Victor caught her with the cool air of a Chinese-American boy.

Jennifer was attracted to Victor not just because he was handsome, but because he was a handsome *Asian* guy. Somehow she felt that he carried some exotic quality by his being Asian alone, though she knew he was as American as any one of his white guy friends. Victor had the exotic appeal of the East without actually having the other unattractive cultural baggage such as a Chinglish accent (of an F.O.B.), geeky clothes, and wimpy personality. Victor knew what Jennifer wanted, and he played to her stereotype.

That night Victor could not sleep but lay in bed with his eyes wide open. He had already masturbated once, but he still wasn't tired. He thought of his cousin and felt guilty. Victor had been making an effort to extract his cousin's image out of his masturbation fantasy.

Because Edward was his ideological enemy, he felt the necessity to resist. In order for him to be normal, he must view his older cousin as the other. He must not be too sympathetic because he feared he might give in and get sucked into the other side. Yet for these couple of days, he had been changing his mind about his need for a pure normal self. He realized that he could do things that would remain undiscovered as long as nobody knew. He could no longer contain the intense animosity of lust.

When night fell again, Victor told his parents that he was going to the library with a few friends.

At eight o'clock, he called Jennifer from a pay phone on the street and told her that he couldn't make it tonight. They set up a date for tomorrow night.

At eight forty, Victor parked his car on Van Ness. He walked down a desolate side street with his hands in his pockets.

Standing at a street corner beside a fire hydrant, Victor lit a cigarette. He was nervous, but he told himself that no one would recognize him. No one knew who he was. He was completely anonymous. He had even made up a name for himself. He sucked his cigarette, blew out a cone of smoke and squinted. He eyed the passersby in the shadow of his baseball cap. He was beginning to get looks.

Before he finished the first cigarette, a car pulled to a stop beside him. The man within rolled down the window on the passenger side. He was, of course, unattractive. Suddenly, Victor felt intimidated. He did not know what to say.

"Hi," said the man.

"Hi," replied Victor.

"Get in. We'll talk."

Hesitantly, Victor got inside the car. The man breathed rather noisily. There was a wheezing sound every time the man inhaled. The man drove slowly up Polk and turned off onto a quiet side street. He stopped the car beside the curb but left the engine running.

"So what's your name?" asked the man.

"Jason."

"How much do you want, Jason?"

"I'm not sure."

"And what do you do, Jason?"

"I don't do anything."

"I see."

Silence.

"I'll give you a fifty if you let me suck your dick. What do you say?"

"You're not kidding me, are you?" says Edward, somewhat shocked, facing the now silent Victor. "I mean... how long have you been doing this?"

"For some time." Pause. "I stopped after I came out to you." Victor picks up the cup of tea on the floor and takes a sip. It's cold.

"More tea?"

"I'm fine," says Victor and takes another sip of cold tea.

"You've been safe, haven't you?"

"I let them blow me, and I let them touch me. I didn't have to do a thing. I got myself off and went home. I woke up in the morning and went to school. No one would know about it, and I could probably live the rest of my life like that." Pause. "Then again maybe not."

"Why did you decide to come out to me?"

"Because... I don't know."

"Do you still consider yourself bisexual?"

"I don't know what I am, Edward."

Edward nods lethargically, hypnotized by Victor's experience. He cannot help feeling impressed, and somewhat smug. After all, Victor isn't as untainted as Edward thinks. They are now on more equal footing.

"Edward, I know you went through a hard time, but I did too. I wasn't attracted to those ugly men. I just needed to get off, and I couldn't help it. And you know, it gets harder and harder to act normal. I mean... to pretend I'm still straight."

"A lot of rationalization."

Victor nods, and drops his head slightly. Edward hugs him. They remain on the futon for some time in silence.

"I told them I'm spending the night at your place," says Victor as he replaces the receiver.

"They'll suspect."

"No," says Victor and sits beside Edward. "How can they suspect? That I'm fucking my own cousin? They can't possibly imagine that."

"Just what if, hypothetically speaking, they find out?"

"Let's go to bed."

Edward and Victor strip naked and nestle together under the comforter, their erections touching each other. Edward's hardened penis still feels the post-ejaculation drain from earlier in the day.

After sex, they lie still. A cold draft brushes Edward's chest. He pulls the comforter over their bodies. Victor turns around and lies on his stomach. Edward climbs over him and sits on the arch between the end of his cousin's spine and the beginning of his ass. His hands touch the smooth skin stretching over the lean back and start pushing his palms against the sides of the spine in a circular motion.

"It feels good," says Victor.

The telephone rings. Edward hops off Victor and scrambles to pick up the phone.

"What are you doing?" It's David.

"I'm about to go to sleep," says Edward, feeling a sudden discomfort. "Victor is spending the night over."

"I see."

"Did you see Ricardo?"

"Yeah, I did."

"So we're still going on the AIDS walk on Saturday."

"Yeap."

Edward gets off the phone after a few more uninformative lines of exchange. His nose is runny now. He returns to the warmth under the blanket, beside his cousin's body. In silence, Edward secretly negotiates his guilt. If David didn't call, would he still feel the same way? Why should he feel guilty? They are not in a monogamous relationship.

"Are you okay?" asks Victor in a quiet, almost intimidated voice.

"Yeah," says Edward and hugs him.

"You love him, don't you?"

"I don't know what love is."

"I don't either, but you care a lot for him."

"I guess I do."

"You think about him a lot."

"I guess so."

"What do you think about me?"

"I'm sexually attracted to you," says Edward after a long pause. "You're my cousin. I'll always love you."

"It's different."

"Yeah. Different from how I feel about Dave, because Dave and I don't have any blood tie. I guess there's this illusion that I can lose him so much easier because our relationship is completely independent of the family."

"But you think that our blood tie actually makes that much of a difference?"

"Yes, because we're Chinese. We were brought up to value our blood tie."

"But if I don't like you, I won't even bother to be your friend. I told you before, didn't I?"

"Still, we grew up together. We have so much more history than what Dave and I have. That's why I feel my relationship with him is much more fragile and insecure. It's not that I don't care about you or love you. I'm just saying that it's different. I don't know. That's just how I feel now. At this moment."

"You know, Edward, you're strange, but in a cool way." Victor adds hesitantly, "And you're my cousin. I know I would have been very different, perhaps more normal, if you weren't around."

"Do you hate me for it?"

"I don't mean 'normal' in a bad way. You made me think about a lot of things differently."

"You know what's weird?" asks Edward with a smile. "Dave said the same thing. So I guess I function as this bizarre agent of ideological subversion."

"On your intellectual high horse again?"

"Sometimes that's all I have to protect myself. Being intellectual gives me more distance to things. Also, being intellectual is a more democratic form of elitism that is not based on an inborn exteriority, you know, like looks and money—"

"But you can make money too."

"Fine, but being intellectual is more mobile because education is already democratized in our society."

"That's not true. What about people who are born stupid?"

"I don't believe that."

"But education still requires money. I don't think poor kids get the same education that wealthy kids do."

"That's a valid point."

"How did we get into this?" asks Victor with a sleepy laugh.

"I forgot." Edward yawns. "I'm cold."

They nestle together for more warmth.

"Can't you turn on the heater?"

"If I do, it gets real hot in the middle of the night. It's like waking up in hell. I'd rather put on another layer of blanket."

"Are you that cold?"

"I'm fine now."

"I miss sleeping with you," says Victor.

"Me too."

They shift positions. Edward lies sideways. Victor tucks his knees behind Edward's. Victor folds an arm around Edward's chest and closes his eyes.

"Do you think we can really be in love with each other?" Victor's words transform into warm breaths on the follicles behind Edward's neck.

"I don't expect you to get so mushy."

"Bitch."

"Misogynist."

Victor laughs.

Edward:

Originally I wanted to write you, but I decided to send you a cassette tape because I want to spare you from reading Chinese. I don't know how much Chinese you read. I just cannot envision you writing Chinese.

I spoke briefly with your mother after you left. She seemed to care a lot about you. Sometimes perhaps you just have to argue less with her.

We'll be having the phone lines installed in two weeks. Everything is coming together. I don't know if you know Jack, but he left the organization because he didn't get along with Perry. Jack is starting his own gay organization.

Jack probably thought Perry was too authoritative. How's David? And your cousin? Kenneth and I broke up. He's back to his ex-boyfriend.

I'm gonna have to stop for a minute.

Anyway, I'm not seeing anyone now. You remember that day we spent together. I guess I did kind of want it, and I guess you did too, but I held back because... because you're leaving and I know I would have missed you really badly if we had done anything...

The cassette goes on. Edward listens to Simon's story while he is sweating on the Stairmaster. He is somewhat happy that Simon has admitted that he liked Edward. It was mutual. When Simon runs out of things to talk about, he plays a song. Then his voice returns.

Edward has finished both sides of the cassette by the time he finishes his workout. He approaches the water fountain and drinks from it. Sweat drops cling unsteadily onto his forehead. He glances at his reflection in the mirror for a second, and leaves the fitness room.

Swimmers are practicing outside under the afternoon sun. Edward stands near the window, where he has a good view of the pool. He watches their smooth strokes, so effortless and at ease, slicing through the water.

Edward swam for one year. He had tried hard to train himself, but he could never attain the ease of these swimmers. He was always struggling for breaths. When he caught a cold near the end of that year, he switched from swimming to exercising on the Stairmaster.

Once, this young political science professor (a self-glorified rice queen) tried to pick Edward up in the shower. Edward ended up having dinner with him but kept a skeptical distance. He was nice enough, intelligent enough, but Edward was not attracted to him.

The shower is empty now. Edward turns the tap and waits for the water to get warm. He feels his chest, which has grown more muscular since freshman year. His body has grown. He shampoos his hair, soaps his body and his face. He realizes that it's already March. A few hours ago, he received a letter from UCLA notifying him that he has made the first cut for the film program. He would have to go down to Los Angeles for an interview.

His stomach is empty. Edward enjoys this feeling. There is a perverse beauty in starvation and anorexia. He often jokes about anorexia as a form of cultural resistance. His legs are sore from exercising. Walking to Ellen's house, he passes by Yogurt Park where he works and picks up a small frozen yogurt.

Ellen is blow-drying her hair when Edward arrives at her apartment. She tastes a spoonful of Edward's frozen yogurt and continues to blow dry her hair.

"I got an interview at UCLA," says Edward.

"That's so great!" says Ellen. "I think you have a really good chance. How many people are they accepting?"

"Sixteen out of the fifty."

"I think you'll get in."

"I hope so." Edward sinks to silence and turns on the television. He flips through the channels.

"Is Dave driving you down to L.A. for the interview?"

"Yeah, we talked about it briefly. He said he would go."

"Great." Ellen starts to put foundation on her face, smoothing it over her skin with her fingers.

"I had a ménage à trois last night."

"With whom?"

"Dave, Victor and me."

"Oh, my God."

"You know, it's getting kind of strange because I don't know who I'm seeing anymore."

"So was it fun?"

"It was a little awkward in the beginning, but then it got better. We slept together in my apartment."

"That is really bizarre." Ellen starts to laugh. "I just can't imagine the kind of cultural taboo that you flirt with. Are you happier with your relationships now?"

"I don't know. I don't want an exclusive relationship. I want to somehow bring everyone together, so there is no reason for jealousy or miscommunication."

"But you seem very skeptical about it."

"I guess I'm *reasonably* happy. Victor can never legitimately be my lover because he's my cousin."

"But heterosexual people marry their cousins, don't they?"

"That's not exactly the point. Victor has always been kind of there. I mean I can't get rid of him as easily as I can get rid of Dave."

"But weren't you in love with your cousin for the longest time?"

"Yeah, but it's different."

"But do you love Dave?"

"I don't know."

"And your cousin now?"

"I love him like I've always loved him. It's a kind of a kinship love. The difference is perhaps that the sex intensifies the relationship a little more." Pause. "But still, I'm not happy because I don't feel secure enough."

"But isn't that the nature of non-monogamous relationships? They'll always be insecure because there's no commitment."

"I guess," says Edward sadly, exhausted of discourse.

"If you have to choose an exclusively committed relationship between either Dave or your cousin, who will you choose?"

"See, it isn't really possible. I don't think Dave likes me enough or I like him enough to... I don't know. And my cousin is sexually ambiguous. In fact, both of them are sexually ambiguous. That by itself makes me very insecure."

"Then it's not worth it to put so much thought into them. If they leave, fuck them. You'll find someone better. By that time, everything you suffered will become negligible."

"But they're all I have *now*."

That Saturday, David, Edward, Ricardo and two other friends went to the AIDS walk. Ricardo and Edward were friendly to each other. They chatted, rather superficially but amiably. When the walk was finished, Edward, Ricardo and David headed off to a mid-day rave in a clearing inside Golden Gate Park. Two loud speakers were set up and blasting techno music. David and Ricardo danced together, like ravers did. Edward was reading Edward Said's *Orientalism* under a tree. Every now and then, he would lift his eyes from the page and see the ravers dance and lounge around.

Edward had learned to tolerate the rave scene since David liked to rave. Nevertheless, he remained skeptical since Edward heard that two of his gay friends went to a rave where some teenagers yelled "faggots" and spat at them.

By the time they were on the BART back to Berkeley, Edward could hardly stay awake. He sprawled on the seat facing Ricardo and David. It was at that time that Edward sensed a certain hostility from Ricardo. But Edward was too tired to analyze. When they got out of the BART station, Ricardo was eager to part with Edward and David.

Later that night, Edward and David went to a dinner party together. Afterward, Edward dropped David off on campus since David was to visit Ricardo at the studio. David kissed Edward goodnight and got out of the car.

David walked toward Kroebar Hall where Ricardo, an architecture major, was working in his studio space. The half moon was hanging in the deep blue and starless sky. David's stomach was full, and he felt satisfied—both sexually and emotionally.

He stepped into the silent foyer of Kroebar Hall and pressed the button for the elevator. There was nothing but silence, light and shadows of still objects. Ricardo was sitting by the drafting table when David knocked on the door. He opened the door for David. The telephone in the hallway rang. Ricardo ran to answer it.

It wasn't for him.

David took off his jacket and sat on the chair, awaiting Ricardo's return. Ricardo hung up and walked casually back into his studio and closed the door.

"You didn't tell me the whole story, did you?" asked a cold voice.

"What whole story?"

"That night when you slept with Edward."

"Of course we had sex."

"Of course you had sex?"

Ricardo let out a breath and leaned against the wall. David got up and approached Ricardo hesitantly. He cast his eyes on the floor for a second, and looked at Ricardo whose face was mangled by hostility.

"I thought we had something special. You know, the whole trip we went on together. I mean the sex we had was so different," said Ricardo, somewhat desperately.

"But I already told you I didn't want an exclusive relationship from the beginning," said David softly.

"All I'm saying is that I thought we had something special."

"I'm sorry. I thought I made it clear."

With a snort, Ricardo walked toward his drafting table. He started to tidy it up a little.

"You make me feel kind of sick," said Ricardo. "I can't have sex with you anymore."

"Okay, if that's what you want."

Ricardo continued to arrange things on his desk. Stacking the drawings together. David stood watching Ricardo's back, half angry and half frustrated. The silence was becoming painfully hostile.

"Do you want me to go?" asked David.

"If you want."

"I'll call you tomorrow or something."

"Whatever."

David called Ricardo the day after, but Ricardo sounded cold on the phone. David thought if that was what Ricardo wanted he was ready to give up their relationship. It wasn't fair for him to try so hard when it wasn't really his fault in the first place.

"So do you want to see a movie?"

"If you want to," said Ricardo.

It wasn't the sex that mattered; it was their friendship. David didn't want to lose a friend.

David and Ricardo met at the cinema and went in together. They spoke of casual things: school, work and mutual friends. David felt very stifled because he could not tell him anything that vaguely involved Edward. He feared that Ricardo would get angry. Indeed, he would.

Later, he asked Edward, "You're not upset when I talk about Ricardo, are you?"

"Of course not," said Edward.

A few times Edward saw Ricardo on the street. Edward would always wave and act as if nothing had happened. Ricardo would throw Edward a strained smile or a brief acknowledgment. Whenever a convenient distance was present, Ricardo would avoid Edward completely. By and by, they got used to passing and ignoring each other.

A week before the interview at UCLA, Edward receives an offer from Yale. He didn't expect to get into Yale, but he did. He is tempted to postpone film school for another year so that he can finish his one-year M.A. degree at Yale. Ellen hugs Edward hard when he breaks the news to her. She is more than positive that Edward will make it into film school.

Edward receives congratulations from almost everyone except his two lovers. Victor says, "That's cool." David's response is no more than a "Hm."

On the Friday afternoon before the interview, David and Edward drive down to Los Angeles. On the way, they pass a valley on whose green slopes stand windmills resembling aliens from old science-fiction movies. Some are turning, and some aren't.

While David is driving, Edward puts a hand on David's crotch and feels the erection grow. David's eyes are focused on the road. He unzips David's shorts and releases the erect penis through the opening on his briefs. He examines the paleness of David's penis, and recalls the darker complexion of Victor's.

When David's penis gets soft, Edward starts playing with it again. It hardens.

"Stop it," says David.

"It's fun," says Edward with a smile and licks David in the ear.

David puts his penis back inside his briefs and zips up his shorts. Just as Edward reaches over to touch him, David catches Edward's hand and kisses it.

On the first night, Edward and David stay at the house of an eccentric gay independent filmmaker. Edward met him from an organization where he used to work as an intern one summer. The two younger men sleep together on the floor of the living room. Edward cannot sleep throughout the night. He listens to David's noisy breathing. He cannot stop thinking about Victor or the interview.

Edward is slightly disappointed that he didn't talk to Victor before he left. Is he paranoid? Victor has been acting nonchalant and cold.

It's about eight o'clock in the morning. Edward is wide awake. He does not know how much he has slept. Though he remembers dreaming about Victor briefly, he has already forgotten what the dream is about.

David is still sleeping.

When Edward opens his eyes again, it's already ten o'clock and he is lying alone. He gets up and walks into the kitchen, where David is having breakfast with the older man.

"Good morning," says Edward.

"Would you like some breakfast?" asks the older man kindly.

They park the car on the UCLA campus and walk to Westwood. The interview is only two hours away. David holds Edward's hand. They wander aimlessly and end up in a café. Edward feels drained, though he isn't sleepy. He orders a cappuccino and pours a pack of Equal in it. David sits silently across Edward at the table.

"Are you nervous?" asks David.

"A little. More or less." Pause. "I kind of want to go to Yale for a year and then go to film school."

Alone now, Edward walks back on campus for the interview. His heartbeat increases as he approaches Melnitz Hall. Following signs, he finds the room where he is supposed to be interviewed. Outside the room, a white woman with an English accent asks him his name and tells him to wait.

David will meet him again outside in an hour's time.

Edward wants to go to film school, doesn't he? That's what he has been planning to do since he was twelve. His mood is ambivalent. His thoughts become more and more scattered. About the future. About what he wants to do. About David. About Victor. About endings and beginnings. About film school. About Yale.

"Mr. Ng?" interrupts the voice of the English woman.

She leads Edward inside the interview room where three middle-aged white men are sitting in lazy poses. Edward shakes hands with each of them.

"This is Professor Jacobi," says one of the white men, "this is Professor Silverman, and I'm Professor Willis."

Somewhat tense, Edward sits before the three men. His hands rest on the table. Edward's heart is pounding. He is disappointed and very *othered* by their age and whiteness.

"We've read your application, and of course, we're interested in your work, otherwise you wouldn't be here," says Willis.

"What we are here for," says Silverman, "is for *you* to tell us something interesting about yourself so we can get to know you better. It's also an opportunity for you to ask questions so you can get to know *us* better."

"We want to see your passion," adds Jacobi.

"Passion," says Edward after a short pause between their words and his silence, "I mean the discourse of passion is already so banalized in our culture. It's not that I don't believe in passion, but rather, I think, to be a filmmaker or an artist is more of a necessity than passion. And this necessity I always take as an assumption that I don't question. As you know, I want to make films that..."

Completely passionless and rational, Edward continues to spill his words. It is as if his blood has dried up. The three men listen with their solemn faces, unmoved lips and focused eyes on the young man whom they find incomprehensible.

"We want you to show us your passion," repeats one of the professors who thinks that Edward has drifted off the topic.

Toward the end of the interview, Edward asks the professors some bureaucratic questions about the program. It will last about four years, extremely liberal: one that "would allow you to explore all venues of the art."

Edward gets up from the chair, shakes hands with the professors and walks out of the office.

Under the sepia complexion of the smog-covered sky, David stands with his hands in his shorts' pockets outside the building. David's face appears so benign, so comforting. Edward hugs David and closes his eyes. He feels David's arms around him.

"I did a really mediocre job," says Edward.

"I'm sure you did fine." David strokes Edward's hair.

"No, I was so mediocre. When I walked into the room and saw three heterosexual white men sitting there with their smug faces, I just thought why the hell would I want to come to this school. You know what I mean? I just don't feel that they have the right to judge me."

David leans his head against Edward's shoulder. They trudge toward the garage, holding each other's hand.

They were making love at Jennifer's apartment that night. He kissed her. She unbuttoned his shirt, and then his fly. Victor's penis was semi-erect. Jennifer closed her lips around it. Victor closed his eyes and saw his cousin sucking him. His organ continued to grow. Fragmented images from the ménage à trois returned to his mind.

When Victor opened his eyes, he saw Jennifer's face. She opened her mouth and kissed Victor. They lay on top of each other. Victor felt her erect nipple and started sucking on it. The foreplay was approaching an end.

"Do you have condoms?" asked Victor.

"I don't think so," said Jennifer.

"Me neither."

"But I'm on the pill."

"I don't think it's safe."

"You don't trust me?"

"No, it's not that."

"It's okay," said Jennifer seductively and touched Victor's already softening penis. She gave it a few strokes. It was still a little soft. He kissed her to distract her focus on his phallus.

"What's wrong?"

"I just think we should start practicing safe sex."

"No, that's not it," said Jennifer and sat up on the bed. Victor did the same, his shoulder touching hers.

"Are you seeing another girl?" asked Jennifer with a very calm voice.

"No," said Victor.

"I can feel there's something wrong," said Jennifer. "It's really okay as long as you tell me."

Victor sank into silence, and for a moment, he was tempted to confess.

"I know you've slept with somebody else before, and you didn't tell me about it. That's okay, I told myself. If you didn't want to let me know, then that's really not my business." Pause. "Do you not trust me, Victor? Still?"

"I'm not sleeping with another girl."

"All right, fine," said Jennifer, somewhat exasperated. She stood up and walked toward the mirror. She put her finger over her right nipple and examined its reflection briefly. Then she picked up the bra on the floor and put it on.

"I'm sorry I'm just not in the mood," said Victor, "I mean it's really nothing to do with you."

Victor pulled up his underwear and put on his jeans. Jennifer threw on a T-shirt. She looked at the pretty Asian boy sitting on her bed looking somewhat distraught.

"Are you bored of me?" asked Jennifer.

"No. Are you?"

"I love you," said Jennifer sharply. "I guess I have never seriously told you that."

"I love you too," said Victor, even though he knew he did not love her. He said it because she wanted to hear it.

After they got dressed, they went out for coffee. Victor was holding Jennifer's hand while they were walking on the San Francisco street. They walked into a café at the Opera Plaza. The Asian boy and the white girl sat at a table. They each ordered a cup of cappuccino and a slice of cheesecake. Jennifer looked at Victor with a smile. She seemed to have forgotten about the rather awkward sex an hour before.

"You're beautiful," said Victor.

"Thank you," said Jennifer with a smile.

Amidst their conversation, Victor felt an intense alienation that he could not describe. He was sitting in front of the perfect girlfriend, yet he felt so lonely and silenced.

Victor drove Jennifer home. She invited him to stay over, but Victor casually declined the offer. They kissed each other good-bye. Driving on the highway, Victor passed by the junction to Bay Bridge. By the time he decided to take the exit, he had already passed it. He drove on.

Home.

The front door opened. Victor entered and locked it behind him. His father was sitting before the television in the living room. He took off his Cal cap that Edward bought him and smoothed his hair.

"You're back?" asked his father in Cantonese.

"Yeah," said Victor in English. "Did anyone call, Dad?"

"I'm not sure. Ask your mother." His father wiped his face with his hand and let out a yawn. "Who did you go out with?"

"Jennifer."

"She's a hot babe, isn't she?" said his father with a smile.

"Yeah," said Victor. "I think I'm going to bed."

Linda had just finished loading the dishes inside the dishwasher when Victor entered. He sat at the kitchen table. She poured a cup of tea for herself and sat with her son.

"Did you have fun?" asked his mother.

"Yeah," said Victor. "Did anyone call?"

"Your cousin called. He left a message earlier in the day."

Victor was relieved.

"How is he doing?" asked his mother.

"He's going down to L.A. for an interview for film school."

"So that's what he plans to do with his life?"

"He also got into Yale."

"Yale?"

"He isn't sure if he'll go because he's quite set to go to film school."

"Yale. My God. It's hard to believe."

"He's always very smart."

"I don't doubt that."

"But you do." Victor hesitated. He continued after a short pause, "He's not that weird. I think a lot of people misperceive things that he does. He has gone through a lot." He sees his mother has already lost interest in the topic.

"I certainly hope he'll do well and have a happy life. He's part of the family too, when he doesn't try so hard to make himself strange."

That night, Victor was alone in bed. He turned and shifted under the blanket. He couldn't help but think about Edward. He couldn't help being anxious about his decision. He couldn't bear the naming of his desire. Hustling was one thing; it was an act of socio-sexual rebellion. But being gay was so naked, so personal, so unnamable.

In the morning, around ten o'clock, he called Edward's apartment but reached the answering machine. He realized that Edward had already left for Los Angeles, or perhaps he was still at David's apartment.

Victor hung up without leaving a message.

Later on that day, he had lunch with his parents in a Chinese restaurant. Victor was conscious that he was playing a role. It was alienating and painful. But his parents could not detect anything. While he felt smug being the flawless actor, he secretly desired that his parents would find out about the truth.

"Do you know Chung Tuck got into Yale?" the wife asked her husband.

"He got into Yale?"

"He did," affirmed Victor.

"Good for him then," said his father coldly. "Have you heard from Berkeley and Stanford about your transfer yet?"

"No, not yet. But should be pretty soon," said Victor.

"How's Jennifer?" asked his mother.

"She's fine."

"Why don't you invite her over for dinner some time?" suggested his mother.

"Just leave them alone," said his father. "They're young adults now."

"I'm just making an offer," said the wife, slightly offended by her husband's belittling comment.

"I'm sure she'd love to," said Victor, knowing well that ultimately he had nothing to lose because he did not love Jennifer. She was no more than a piece of jewelry on his body.

Funky psychedelic images flash across the walls of the warehouse with techno music at an ear-blasting volume. Edward and David are dancing before each other. Yet another rave: Wacky Citrus. David is happily dancing, wearing a pair of orange ski goggles. Edward dances, watching the other bodies writhing around him in the high of ecstasy and acid.

Every time when David asks Edward if he is having fun, Edward always says "Yeah." Though David senses Edward's insecurity, he stops second-guessing Edward's words. He can't be expected to be a mind reader, can he?

"That's Victor," says Edward amidst the pulse-pounding beat.

A puzzled expression appears on David's face. Edward leans toward David and shouts into David's ear. "Wait here," says Edward, "I'll go say hi."

His eyes follow Victor's face amidst a sea of bouncing heads. Edward squeezes through the sweaty bodies. Victor stands with Jennifer before a wall, surveying the dancers. He does not notice Edward's approach until Edward waves his hand in front of his eyes.

"What's up?" asks Edward with a smile.

"I tried calling you," says Victor.

"When?"

"Last Saturday."

"I was in L.A."

"I figured." Pause. "This is Jennifer."

"Hi," says Edward. He awkwardly shakes hands with the girl.

Edward exchanges a few sentences with Victor, parts with them and squeezes back into the dancing crowd.

Before the mesmerized David, Edward dances. He begins to get depressed. They stop dancing, drift to a quieter corner and sit on the floor. David unzips his backpack and takes out a pack of Nilla cookies. He offers

Edward some, but Edward shakes his head with a smile. David eats a few cookies and replaces the box of cookies into his knapsack.

"What's wrong?"

"I'll tell you later," says Edward.

At five o'clock in the morning, the warehouse has become a refugee camp. Edward sits alone on the floor scattered with bubble gum wrappers, trampled flyers, plastic cups and other garbage. Victor has probably left.

Around six o'clock, Edward is in the car with David driving. They are crossing the Bay Bridge back to Berkeley. Edward's clothes smell of smoke.

The sun is rising.

The silence is comforting after hours of pulse-pounding techno music. The ski goggles are hanging loosely under David's chin. Edward looks out of the window. He shuts his eyes. He is sick of the Bay Bridge, of the crossing.

"Victor hasn't called me for a whole week," says Edward. "And now I saw him with his girlfriend at a rave."

David strokes Edward's thigh gently.

"Why does he drop in and out of my life like that? I just feel..." Edward doesn't know what to say.

"I'm sorry," says David.

"It's not your fault," says Edward. "You're not jealous when I talk about Victor, are you?"

"Of course not."

"But you know what's strange? I kind of expected this to happen. I just— just couldn't imagine he could actually come out."

"Hm."

"It's depressing that people are so predictable."

Silence. David affixes his sleepy gaze ahead.

"I'm sorry. I'm boring you."

"I'm just tired."

The car stops beside the curb. The engine dies. They get out of the car and confront the early morning chill that zeroes Edward's spine. Sniffling, Edward trudges beside David toward the apartment building. David unlocks the front gate, and they go inside.

Sun rays creep through the uncovered margins around the curtains that David just closed. Naked, he walks toward the bed with his beautiful skinny legs, sits on the bed and scratches his head.

"Do you want to go to sleep?" he mumbles and yawns.

"Sure," says Edward softly and unbuttons his jeans.

Edward wakes up and looks at the clock. It's almost noon. He closes his eyes again beside the sleeping David.

The ringing telephone wakes David. He dashes off the bed, leaving Edward confused with his eyes just opened. Edward opens his eyes and catches David's words outside. He looks at the clock: it's already two in the afternoon. David's naked figure enters the room once again and hops onto the bed beside Edward.

"Who's that?" asks Edward.

"It's for my roommate." David pulls the blanket over his chilled body. He looks at Edward who remains dazed and confused with his hand bracing his leaden head.

"Are you still upset about your cousin?" asks David.

"No," says Edward. "Maybe I'm a little sad."

David touches Edward's smooth thigh and reaches for Edward's flaccid penis. It hardens.

"I think I'll go to Yale," says Edward. "It'll be different."

"Cool." David kisses Edward and holds Edward's hand. "I haven't told you. But I'm very proud of you."

Victor left the rave about an hour after he saw Edward. He drove Jennifer back to her apartment. He tried thinking of whatever could turn him on when he was fucking her. When he opened his eyes again, his semen had already filled the condom. He kissed her.

Later, she was sleeping in his arms. Her blond hair spread over his shoulder. She slept, while Victor's eyes remained open.

They were having waffles around eleven o'clock that morning. Jennifer smiled. He found her face so cinematic. The golden syrup stayed stubbornly at the mouth of the jar. Victor held the handle and shook the jar. A golden string of syrup fell slowly in the air.

"Coffee?" asked Jennifer with a smile.

"That'll be great."

Jennifer got up. Her slim legs strutted toward the kitchen counter. She ground some coffee beans, poured them into the filter, and switched on the coffee machine.

"More waffles?"

"I'm fine," replied Victor. Thanks."

She opened the freezer door and threw the box of the waffles inside.

"Do you think my cousin is cute?" asked Victor.

"Your cousin?" asked Jennifer.

"The guy who came up to me last night."

"Oh. He's your cousin? I didn't quite catch his name. It was so loud." She realized she forgot to plug in the coffee machine. So she plugged it in. "What was your question?"

"Do you think my cousin is cute?"

"He's okay," said Jennifer matter-of-factly. "I guess he's kind of cute, in a boyish way."

"He's gay."

"Oh." Jennifer took out two coffee mugs from the pantry. "He's gay?"

"But he's cool."

"I have some gay friends too. They're all so sweet and intelligent."

Victor poured some more syrup onto the remaining corner of his waffle. He pushed the fork into the crusty piece and put it in his mouth. A few wisps of steam evaporated quickly from the surface of the hot coffee. Victor added cream and sugar. He remembered a line from Spike Lee's film *Malcolm X* which went something like: *The only thing that I integrate is my coffee.*

She sat before Victor with a cup of coffee between her palms. If Jennifer had been Asian, would Victor have gone out with her? Playing with the salt bottle, she asked matter-of-factly, "Do you talk to your cousin much?"

"Sometimes. We grew up together."

"Is it hard for you to accept that he is gay?"

"It was a little strange at first, I suppose. We became more distant. I guess there's a lot of homophobia on my part too."

"I kind of like gay friends. I feel comfortable around them because they're... not threatening. You know what I mean? It's just like I'm with one of my girl friends." She took a sip of coffee and mused on, somewhat romantically. "I find their life kind of tragic. They have to face all the discrimination and hatred."

"I'm sorry. I don't know what else to say."

"Don't be sorry. It's your life, Victor. Whatever you want to do with it is your own problem."

"Are you angry?"

"Does it matter if I'm angry?"

Silence.

"You have Dave."

"You have Jennifer too."

"I think I really love her."

"Cool."

"You don't believe me."

"Of course I do." Edward tightens his grip on the receiver.

"Let's be friends, Edward."

"I'm your cousin, right?"

"Right."

Edward's voice is gone. Victor slowly replaces the receiver of the pay phone. The hallway is desolate and quiet. Victor shoulders his knapsack and heads toward the bathroom.

Colorless piss splashes against the glistening bleached wall of the urinal. A man unzips himself and pulls out his fat penis beside Victor. As Victor zips up his jeans, he catches the glimpse of an erect penis. The man, thirtyish, white, slightly fat, is smiling at Victor.

Victor returns a smile and walks into a cubicle. Keeping cool, Victor waits inside. A knock on the cubicle's door. Victor lets the man inside. He unzips himself and takes out his hard cock. Without negotiation, the man sinks down on his knees and takes Victor's penis into his mouth. While sucking Victor, the man takes out his own erection from his pants and jerks himself off. Closing his eyes, Victor hears the sucking noise. He imagines the man to be someone else.

Someone else apart from Edward.

As soon as Edward enters his mind, Victor opens his eyes. Dazed, he looks down and watches the man suck his penis.

Minutes pass. The man is still sucking. Victor no longer feels pleasure. He is overwhelmed with a sense of loss. Jets of white semen spurt against Victor's jeans. The man has come. He sucks on. Another minute passes. The man stops sucking and looks up at Victor.

"I can't come," says Victor softly.

The man zips himself up and leaves the cubicle. His penis is soft now. He wipes it dry with toilet paper, sticks the thing back into his fly and sits on the toilet. With masses of toilet paper, he wipes away the drying semen that threatens to form a crusty discolored patch on his jeans.

It was almost two o'clock in the morning on the day that Edward was to move away from his uncle's house. Edward and Victor lay awake on their beds in darkness. In their silence was a faint electric drone from the lamps outside.

"I'll miss you, Victor," said Edward.

"Are you excited about Berkeley?"

"Yeah. In a way." Edward's eyes were tearful.

"Are you cold?" asked Victor.

"No, I'm all right." A teardrop fell down his cheek. He couldn't wipe it, because the motion of his shadow would give him away.

"You should be happy. You're leaving at last. Isn't that what you've always wanted?"

"I am happy." Edward closed his eyes to clear the tears covering his pupils.

"You should be. You'll do well at Berkeley, then go to film school. Don't forget about me, man."

"You're probably the only person here I care to remember."

"You blame them, don't you?"

"They've done whatever they can for me. I have no complaints. After all, they're not my parents. I'm not part of your family."

"Don't say that. You're always welcome back. You know that." Pause. "Don't you feel free?"

"I guess I do," said Edward. "But I don't know if it isn't as bad out there, or maybe even worse. I'd rather be pessimistic so I can expect the worst."

"That's no way to live, Edward. You got to be more positive."

"But I can't. I'm not a positive person. My dad died when I was six. My mom didn't give a shit about me, so she sent me off to America. I just can't see how I can ever be happy."

A car passed by outside. Its headlights blazed up the room and the shadows shifted.

"You can always count on me."

"I'll see you in Berkeley in two years."

"I hope so."

"We can share an apartment together. It'll be fun." It was Edward's fantasy that never came true. Although he had no model of homosexuality then, he imagined the two of them living together. They would go to school, come home, have dinner together, and perhaps even share the same bed. Edward did not see himself as homosexual, but he had a certain vision.

Near the end of April, Edward receives a rejection letter from UCLA. But he did get into Columbia and USC for film production. Edward has almost made up his mind to go to Yale and reapply to film schools next year, since none of them will grant him a deferral.

"I think you've made the right choice," says Ellen. "You can't really get weaker with a Yale degree. You know what I mean? There's no reason for them not to accept you again next year. You'll continue to work on your videos on the side while you are at Yale."

"And if I decide to stay in Berkeley for another year?"

"For what?" Ellen almost screams.

"I don't know," says Edward with a shrug. He knows, but he feels too ambivalent to articulate it.

"For Dave?"

"Maybe."

"Edward!" Ellen slams her eyebrow pencil down and looks at Edward. "In a year, you'll come back with a Yale degree. Don't stay for Dave. You've known all along that he's just a fling."

"Not exactly a fling."

"But you don't love him. Even if you do love him, he'll understand and won't hold you back. The fact remains that you don't love him, and he doesn't love you. You guys are just fuck buddies."

"I hate to think of it that way," says Edward and lies flat on Ellen's bed covered with feminist books and photocopied articles.

"Think of it this way," says Ellen, "if you stay, he'll really—"

"Despise me."

"Exactly. You give away a great opportunity for a very mediocre relationship that really… you *will* find someone who fits you perfectly. Maybe it will be Dave, but not at this stage of your relationship."

"Yeah. You're always right." Edward knows what is rational. He only feels differently.

"I know the first is always the hardest. The most painful."

"Discounting Victor, he's probably the first guy I've had a most substantial relationship with. You're right. I don't think I really love him. But I can love him, you know, if he is passionate enough, if he really loves me. He just simply won't give me enough passion. It stifles me because I constantly have to check how much I'm feeling for him."

"Go to Yale, Edward, and come back for film school. By then it will give you enough distance from him to be detached, and simultaneously it'll give him more time to mature."

Edward sinks into a ponderous silence.

"Don't take your privilege for granted. Really." Exhausted from persuasion, Ellen picks up her eyebrow pencil and continues lining her eyes.

6

Flight

It was about ten o'clock Hong Kong time. Paulina Clifford got out of the shower and unwrapped the towel around her still graceful waist. She sat before the mirror and started making herself up. She took her time to beautify her face, to cover up the sunburn scars on a side of her cheeks which had been subtly haunting her. She put on her Channel suit and sunglasses.

At almost eleven o'clock, she was in her air-conditioned car. The Filipino chauffeur was steering slowly through the traffic at the Cross Harbor Tunnel. She looked at her Cartier watch. She would be in time for her flight. She asked for the mobile phone, and the chauffeur handed it to her. She called her husband at work and told him that she was leaving. She said "love you" to him and hung up.

Before the first class check-in counter of United Airlines, Paulina flashed out her American passport and paid the airport tax. The young Chinese girl at the counter was typing before the computer keyboard to check Paulina in.

With a nostalgic impulse, Paulina said to the girl in Cantonese, "I once worked for British Airways. It was BOAC then."

"Really." The girl smiled and gave the woman back her American passport. She gave Paulina the gate information and directions in English with such a bad accent that offended Paulina. After all, she was a Hong Kong native, Chinese by descent. What was that girl trying to prove by speaking English?

As the plane took off, Paulina looked out of the window. The elevated view of Hong Kong's heavily constructed landscape moved her. She wondered for how long could she enjoy the luxuries of the colony. Would the Communists "ruin" Hong Kong just as they did once to Shanghai? The stewardess offered her newspapers. Paulina picked a copy of *The San Francisco Chronicle*. She flipped through it briefly and caught the headline about AIDS and HIV vaccines. She saw another article with a photograph of militant gays protesting. She read no more.

"Are you Chinese?" asked a voice beside her in English.

Paulina turned and noticed for the first time the relatively attractive and slim middle-aged Chinese man sitting beside her. His hair was quite white. For a second, she was struck by the prophecy spoken by her fortune-teller: *Beware of men whose hair turned white at their youth.*

"Yes. Are you?" asked Paulina back.

"I thought you were Hong-Kongnese," said the man with a rather charming smile. "I'm sorry that I've disturbed you from reading your paper, but when I saw you, I just couldn't— notice you."

Paulina smiled with reservation.

"What are you going to San Francisco for?" asked the man.

"I'm attending my son's graduation. He's graduating from Berkeley, and he'll be going to Yale."

"You must be very proud. But I just can't imagine that you have a son of that age, because you seem very young."

"I married young."

"Ah. I wouldn't doubt that."

When Paulina got off the plane, the man (named Marcus Hui) offered her a ride. Paulina politely declined, as her son would be picking her up. The man insisted on giving her his phone number in San Francisco. She got her luggage and parted with him.

Her son and another unfamiliar young man were waiting for her outside the gate. Edward introduced David. Paulina heard of that name, and knew that David must be his son's lover. She shook the other boy's hand. He was quite handsome—a mixed-blood boy of Caucasian and Chinese descent. Suddenly, seeing David's face, she remembered the sexualized touch of the man during the darkness on the plane. She thought (or perhaps dreamt) that the man was touching her leg—very sensually—when she was half-asleep.

David didn't talk much. Seated in the back, he answered politely and laconically Paulina's quaint questions. The car stopped beside her brother's house. Both Edward and David carried the luggage for the exquisitely bourgeois woman. The two boys did not stay long in Edward's uncle's house. Edward gave them directions to his graduation on Saturday and left with David after a brief cup of tea. They walked out of the front door holding hands, leaving the three adults behind: Paulina, Linda and their brother/husband at the kitchen table.

"Where's Victor?" asked Paulina.

"At school," replied Linda.

"You really don't know how to raise your son," said her brother.

"Please," said Linda to her husband, "your sister just got off the plane."

"Has he been a big burden to you two? I'm sorry if I had..." said Paulina slightly irritated. "Whatever he turns out to be is part of your responsibility. You had agreed to help me raise him."

"Chung Tuck has been a good boy," said Linda with a smile, then spoke in English, "and you two should accept the way he is. He is not bad."

"He's just a weirdo," replied the man in English.

"He's my son," said Paulina, "and I love him whatever he is. I can't change him, but I still hope he would change."

"If he's happy, leave him be," said Linda.

"What if your son turns out queer?" snorted Paulina.

"It's nothing to do with his years spent here. You're the one who spoiled him," said her brother.

With a sigh, Linda left the kitchen table and took the empty teapot with her. She started boiling some more hot water at the stove, trying to step out of the tedious conflict.

Paulina grabbed a piece of Kleenex and started to soak up the tears brimming down her cosmeticized eyes. She had plastic surgery once in order to have another fold on each of her lids.

"As soon as I get off the plane, I have to be bombarded," said Paulina, switching to Cantonese, and blew her nose. "All I'm saying is that I love him, and I apologize for all the trouble he caused you."

"You think I don't love him?" asked the man horrified. "I've cared for him more than you, his mother, has ever done for him. I treat him just like my son, but there is nothing I can do if he left this house and turned gay. Don't you blame it on me."

The teapot thudded against the table before the two siblings.

"Don't get too excited," said Linda to her husband. "You don't want another heart attack."

"Don't move," says a voice. "Keep your eyes closed."

"I can't believe how good he looks," says another voice.

"Open your eyes and look up."

Edward does as he is told.

"Pretty pretty."

Geena and Suzy (Ellen's Korean neighbors who dress in black 365 days of the year) are making Edward up. Geena is lining Edward's lips while Suzy is searching in her jewelry box for a pair of glamorous earrings. Geena paints Edward's lips with a China-red lipstick as Edward sits still.

"How about this one?" asks Suzy with a pair of pearl clip-ons between her fingers.

"Beautiful," says Edward.

"You're looking good," says Suzy with awe. "I seriously think you can be such a beautiful woman."

Then comes the powder, the mascara, and the blush. Edward looks at himself in the mirror. His reflection spellbinds him. It resembles the face of his imaginary twin sister, or perhaps the photographed face of his mother in her early twenties. Ellen enters wearing a rented black graduation gown that Edward refused to rent. Precisely because his mother and his uncle want to see him in a legitimized costume, Edward has decided to go to the graduation in drag.

"Oh my God, you look really good!" exclaims Ellen. "You're like... the perfect woman. This is just fucking amazing."

Edward stands up with her prosthetic breasts protruding underneath the tight floral print dress. His professor said that during his youthful years at Berkeley students only went to graduation to give their professors a finger. But Berkeley's graduation has become so conservative now.

On the balcony, Ellen stands beside Edward while Geena takes a photograph of them both. Janice, another Korean English graduate, drives by the apartment and picks Ellen and Edward up to the Greek Theater on top of the hill. Thank God for the lift, thinks Edward, the heels (which he bought from Payless Shoe Source) are killing his toes.

The Asian American intellectuals have gathered in a small clique at the backstage of the Greek Theater. They try hard not to stare at Edward, because they refuse to gratify his otherness. But Edward is undeniably an odd sight among the graduates. He is one of the three persons in his class not wearing conventional gowns. Indeed, he is the only one in drag.

Huy, another queer Vietnamese guy, greets Edward with a smile. They hug each other, despite their lack of usual acquaintance. In his solemn black gown, Huy can't help laughing.

"You look really good," says Huy. "I mean it's really great that you're doing this. I wish I could do this. My parents are here. I only came for them."

"I came for them too."

"Your parents are here?"

"My mother, my uncle and my aunt."

"And you're in drag?"

"Exactly. This is my graduation, and I dress however I please."

"You're really something," says Huy with a sweet shake of his head and walks off.

"Is he queer?" Peter whispers in Edward's ear.

"Huy? Of course he's queer."

"I can tell."

"I guess you've developed a pretty good gaydar from hanging out with me," says Edward with a smile. "Are your parents here?"

"Yeah, they should be," says Peter and takes off his nerdy glasses to wipe away the sweat on the bridge of his nose. "Do you have a program?"

"No, do you?"

"Man, I just can't believe you're coming here in drag," mutters a generic English major.

"Blah blah blah," says Edward in a breeze.

"Let's hug each other on stage," says Peter.

"Sure."

David, Larry, Joey and Deana are waiting at the side of the stage with flowers. When Edward approaches among the infinite line of English graduates in black gowns, Larry and Deana hand Edward two bouquets of flowers. David takes pictures as Edward kisses Deana and Joel. Most of the bystanders do not even realize that Edward is 'a man' except for his mother who stands among his friends with a frigid smile. She politely asks Deana to take a photo of "her son" and herself, and hands the white girl the camera.

On stage, Edward takes out his name card from between her fake boobs and hands it to Professor Franco, the MC. The name "Edward Ning" is pronounced as the woman in the floral print dress receives the mock certificate from another professor wearing a tired sheepish smile. Peter hugs Edward. Ellen hugs Edward. Peter hugs Ellen.

At the reception, strawberries and champagne are served. Edward's mother, his uncle, his aunt and Victor stand silently at a corner. Edward is surrounded by his friends as his family approaches. Victor awkwardly holds out his hand to congratulate Edward. Edward embraces Victor instead.

His uncle tells Edward to show up at the Chinese restaurant at six thirty, and leaves with the rest of his kind. He holds onto the unused camera tightly in his sweaty hand.

Half an hour later, Edward parts with his friends after kisses and hugs. Edward and David walk farther and farther away from the peopled part of the campus. Holding Edward's hands, David cannot help finding Edward's feminized body sexually stimulating.

"Hold on," says Edward and takes off the heels. "They're really killing me. Imagine that women have to walk in them all day long. It's just another version of Chinese foot binding."

"Wear my shoes," says David. "I'll wear your heels for a while."

"No, I'll just walk barefoot."

"But you'll tear your pantyhose. I'll be fine wearing those heels for a few minutes."

Edward and David exchange shoes. Edward is somewhat touched. They walk for another block. David takes off the heels and his socks to walk barefoot.

"Are you happy?" asks David.

"No. Why should I be happy?"

"You've just graduated. Don't you feel you've accomplished something?"

"You know me, Dave," says Edward.

"I know. You think that graduation is an arbitrary cultural marker. But I'm happy. I'm happy because I think you've done a lot, and you're my friend."

Edward smiles gingerly.

The make-up melts from Edward's face under the deluge of warm water. He opens his mouth and lets streaks of water flood his mouth. David enters the shower behind Edward and folds his arms around his chest.

"You're like a panther," says David beside Edward's ear.

"A panther?"

"You have such a muscular upper body, a slim waist and limbs."

"A panther."

Grabbing the bar of soap, David starts soaping Edward's abdomen. His other hand descends toward Edward's crotch.

"You're really sexy in that dress," says David.

"So I guess we should have had sex when I was still in drag."

Edward turns around and seals his mouth over David's.

"I like you better now."

"Really?"

Edward and David arrive at six-thirty sharp. The rest of the party has not yet arrived. The two boys sit silently under the bleak lighting in the Chinese restaurant whose walls are decorated with blown-up photos of Hong Kong. The still-alive fish with whitened, bacteria-infected eyes swim over the pile of suffocated ones in a large green tank. Other Berkeley students are sitting around.

The family shows up at last. His uncle sits down and orders food. Victor talks to Edward mundanely and diplomatically. David remains uncomfortably silent, so do Linda and Paulina, who occasionally make ice-breaking remarks. There is tension. His uncle seems easily irritated. Too exhausted to fight, Edward tries to pass the dinner as peacefully as possible. His uncle has ordered a lot of meat plates.

His uncle watches Edward serve David food.

Such a sissy.

"So when are you going to Yale?" asks Paulina.

"We plan to drive across the country in the middle of July. We'll make it to Yale some time before school starts."

"You always have to make me worry," says Paulina.

"Don't worry, Mrs. Clifford," says David, "we're very safe drivers."

"When you hit those hick towns, you two better be more discrete if you don't want to get shot," says his uncle.

"It's not that bad," says Edward.

"Not that bad? Think of what you always do. You always spoil everything and piss everyone off," continues his uncle, slowly building his rage, "just like you ruin your graduation for your family."

"It's my graduation," says Edward.

"Yes, damn well. Next time give us a warning, so we don't have to show up. You really make us feel very ashamed."

"That's your own problem."

"Will you stop throwing your tantrum?" says Paulina in Cantonese. "I'm here for my son's graduation."

"Good, you just had your son's graduation. You let him put shit in front of your nose, and you smell it like flowers."

"I'm leaving," says Edward and gets up.

"You sit down!" His uncle slams the table. "You're so disrespectful. What have you become?" His uncle rises in rage. "Who the fuck do you think you are?"

Victor and the rest watch helplessly.

"Who the fuck do you think you are? That you can criticize my mother, yell at me whenever you want? I apologize for not having informed you that I was going to my graduation in drag. But I didn't invite you to my graduation. You assumed that you were welcome, and you assumed that I should dress in your way." Edward adds. "So go fuck yourself, really, go fuck yourself."

Edward walks out of the restaurant without looking back. He knows that he probably will not step into that restaurant again, though he might still have to see his uncle and family.

Edward sits silently in his own apartment. He hears knocks from the door. He looks through the peephole. It's David. Edward opens the door. David remains silent with his hands in his pockets and enters the apartment. They sit on the bed side by side.

"I'm sorry," says Edward. "I didn't mean to leave you there. I just couldn't control myself."

David holds Edward.

"I should have just been quiet, but I was so fucking pissed."

Edward holds David tight.

Paulina ended up calling the Chinese man in San Francisco who was a recent immigrant from Hong Kong. He took Paulina out shopping one afternoon and had dinner with her the night before she flew back to Hong Kong.

The photographs of her son in drag were in her suitcase. He would remain a stranger to her. They had only exchanged very mundane words and superficial dialogue. Paulina tried to be satisfied, as long as she could still hear his living voice.

Once again, she parted with him.

After going home that evening, Victor called Edward on the phone. It was already one o'clock, and he was alone in his room. The telephone rang for a few times before Edward picked it up.

"Hello?" Edward's voice sounded awake.

"How're you feeling?" asked Victor.

"Why're you calling me?"

"I just want to know if you're fine."

"Well, thanks."

"I'm sorry."

"You just sat there, Victor. You just sat there and did nothing."

"I'm really sorry about Dad. He's my father, you know. He's old and stubborn, and he won't change. So what's the point?"

"Because you really hurt me for not saying a word."

"What am I supposed to say?"

"That you're like me."

"But I'm *not* like you."

"You're one of us more or less, whether you like it or not, Victor. That's how they'll see it. I hate gay people who can't stand up for themselves, not to mention for others. It's as simple as that."

"But I'm not gay."

"There you go," said Edward coldly.

Silence.

"Give me time."

At the moment when Edward has already waited for an hour, he realizes that he and David will only have two more months at Berkeley together. And then they are supposed to be driving off for Yale. He has already booked David's plane ticket from New Haven to Oakland in August, their final parting.

David was supposed to call an hour ago, but he still hasn't. Edward cannot invent any more excuses, because he knows there is none to be invented.

It's midnight. David still hasn't called. Edward starts brushing his teeth. He washes his face. He calls Ellen, but she isn't home. It's a Friday night, isn't it?

Edward strips and crawls into bed. Tightly closing his eyes, he vainly hopes that the phone will wake him.

Cannot fall asleep.

Edward tries not to open his eyes because he is afraid to catch a glimpse of the digital clock. He doesn't want to know what time it is.

Shifting back and forth in bed.

It's one thirty in the morning. Edward has not fallen asleep. He cannot understand why David didn't give him a call when he couldn't make it.

Edward picks up the phone and holds the receiver in his hand. The dial tone goes off. Edward resets the phone and calls the first number that comes into his mind. He waits.

"Good afternoon," says the voice.

"Hi, Grandma," says Edward.

"Chung Tuck," says the benign voice from the other side of the world, "how are you?"

"I'm all right," says Edward.

"What time is it over there? It must be very late. You still haven't gone to bed?"

"No, I'm just reading."

"Don't work too hard. You need sleep too."

"Yeah."

"Are you feeling happier over there?"

"I'm all right."

Grandmother sighs, and says, "I received your letter a week ago. It makes me very worried when you're not happy. Try to be happy, Chung Tuck. Don't think too much."

Edward remembers the card that he sent his grandmother. He jotted down a brief note in the card:

When I'm sad and unhappy, I think of how strong

you are and become ashamed of how petty things

bother me.

"Don't worry, I'm happier," says Edward.

"I love you very much. When you're unhappy, I'm unhappy too. Do you understand, Chung Tuck?"

Edward wakes up in the morning. He realizes that David hasn't called. Just a goddamn phone call. Why should he get so upset over it? Edward will not call David until David calls.

When Edward is packing to leave for the gym, the telephone rings. It is mid-day, and it is David.

"It was really fun last night. We didn't leave the amusement park until I don't know when... The acid I took was so powerful," says David.

"I'm glad you had fun," says Edward, sitting beside the sun-lit window on the couch in David's living room.

"So where do you want to eat?"

"Dave, I got the ticket." Edward opens up his knapsack and hands the ticket to David.

"Great."

"You know if you don't want to go with me, it's fine. But you have to tell me now."

"I want to go," says David.

"I was waiting for you to call last night."

Silence. David looks at Edward, bites his fingernail absent-mindedly, and looks away.

Dark again. The cum is wiped clean from Edward's abdomen. David lies beside Edward and puts an arm around his body.

"You don't have to put up with me, if you don't want to," says Edward.

"Do you think I'm just putting up with you?"

"I don't know."

"I'm with you only because I want to."

"I guess I just want you to know that if you're tired of me, I don't need a neat ending. You know I don't care for that."

"What are you talking about?"

"Happy endings." Edward says, "I won't be here next year, and Ricardo will. If it's better or easier for you, then it's fine for me."

"I don't know what you mean."

"You know what I mean."

"Dave said he's going to come, didn't he?" asks Ellen. "So why this bizarre paranoia of yours?"

"I'm just tired of contrived happy endings, that's all. Look, I won't be here next year, and if he's sick of me now, I don't see why he should continue to put up with me. It will be hypocritical," says Edward.

"Look, he was on acid that night. He stood you up."

"He could have called, couldn't he? There must have been pay phones around. Furthermore, it's not that he forgets about everything when he's on acid. He's still sane, he still functions. It's just a damn excuse."

"Did he go with Ricardo?"

"Yeah."

"Let it pass, Edward. You guys are leaving in a week, right? You aren't driving alone. It's crazy. It's simply out of the question." Sigh. "I wish I could come with you."

"I just think if mediocrity is all there is——"

"I get your point. But think about how much pain you'll have to endure by breaking up now. Just let the trip end your relationship. Both of you will feel better that way. It wouldn't be because one of you initiates it, but rather, the necessity of distance forces you guys to break up."

Two days left. Edward is waiting at the UPS counter with an unspeakable determination. He waits for the UPS clerk to weigh his boxes one by one. It rings up to about a hundred dollars. Edward writes a check and signs it. He pulls it out, realizing how soon this checkbook will be outdated.

It will no longer be California. He tries to feel glad about getting out of Berkeley. He tries to feel excited about Yale and being close to New York. But he feels sad.

"Edward," says a voice beside him.

"Hey, Peter," says Edward.

"When are you leaving for Yale?" asks the Filipino boy wearing his usual attire (baseball cap and Harvard T-shirt), which Edward finds terribly nostalgic.

"The day after tomorrow."

"So is Dave coming with you?"

"Yeah."

They walk out of the post office together, side by side. For a brief moment, they both remember their time spent together: movies, intellectual discussions, lunches, workouts.

"So you'll be staying here for the master's degree?" asks Edward.

"Yeah. I'll get out in a year and go to law school."

"I guess I'll see you when I come back."

"Sometime soon?"

"Probably during the year."

"All right. Good luck."

They look at each other and hug.

"You're crazy," Ellen almost screams. "Why are you doing this? It's insane."

"I'll be fine," says Edward with a smile. "I have my computer with me. I'll write when I'm driving across the country."

"What is he going to say? Don't, Edward. It will be so miserable." Ellen lets out a helpless sigh. "Has he been an asshole?"

"No, just the same." Edward shrugs. "I'll have to deal with it eventually. The only reason for me to not deal with it now is to make the break-up neater."

"That's not the point. The point is that it's just not safe for you to drive across the country alone. Technically it's not sound. Promise me, Edward. Go with Dave. Please."

They hug each other. Ellen's eyes water.

At three o'clock in the afternoon, David gets out of his apartment and walks up the street toward Edward's apartment. He passes by People's Park where the new volleyball court has been built upon. Homeless people are being driven out. The sidewalk is chalked with their anguish: *Fuck UC Berkeley.*

Edward's car is not in the garage. David walks up the back stairs and enters the dark corridor at the end of which stands Edward's apartment door unmoved. He knocks.

"He left," says a voice, somewhat familiar, somewhat relieving.

But it isn't Edward's. David turns around.

"I've been waiting here for an hour already," says Victor standing at the intersection of two corridors behind David.

"Here." Victor approaches and hands David a note. "I took it off the door. For you."

Sorry, Dave. I have to go alone. Please understand.

Have a good summer. I'll call you soon.

"Why did he do that?" says David and falls into a speechless stupor.

Sitting in a café, David is still speechless before Victor. The note is crumpled and soaked with sweat in his palm. Victor is invisible. David only sees the colors—green from trees, blue from sky, white from glares—among the shifting blurred shapes of passing humans.

"Why did he do that?" asks David.

"He's always... unmanageable," says Victor. "That's why I've always been afraid of him. Maybe not really afraid... but threatened."

"Oh, Edward," mutters David under his breath.

At the moment that Edward embarked on the highway, he felt an unbound freedom. He knew well that the pain would come. Not now. Techno music was blasting his ears. He focused his eyes on the road, ahead, forward. He would feel it later, but by then, it would be too late to turn back.

An hour later, he put on a New Order tape. When it played "Bizarre Love Triangle," David and Edward's favorite song, Edward cried. Tears blurred his vision. He wiped his eyes and put on sunglasses.

When Edward was calm again, he stopped for gas. He realized that it was almost three o'clock, the time when David was supposed to meet him and drive off together from Berkeley. He wasn't planning to call David, because he had already left him a note on the door. But he did. He picked up the receiver at the pay phone, put in a few quarters and dialed David's number. He got David's answering machine.

"Dave, it's me." Edward didn't know what to say for a few seconds, and felt his heart opening within him. "I miss you. I'll call you soon."

Edward hung up. He used the bathroom, paid for the gas and bought a cup of coffee. As he got back inside his car, he suddenly realized that he was in love with David.

He felt both sad and happy, and drove.

About the Author

Quentin Lee was born in Hong Kong. He immigrated to Canada and then the U.S. where he attended University of California at Berkeley and Yale University for his B.A. and M.A. in English. He also attended UCLA for his M.F.A. in Film Production. His feature films and television works are available on streaming worldwide.